The Meat Factory - Text copyright © Emmy Ellis 2020
Cover Art by Emmy Ellis @ studioenp.com © 2020

All Rights Reserved

The Meat Factory

Emmy Ellis

SPECIAL THANKS TO NOTRIGHTS
BOOK CLUB

A Word of Advice, Cass

"When I'm gone, my precious little bird, and you take over from your old man, fly with wings of steel and harden your heart to stone, because if you don't, they'll shoot you down and clip your wings, cracking open that stone to expose the softness inside. Don't let them. Keep the softness for those who matter. Always remember the rule, except it'll be in your name instead of mine: *What Cassie says goes.* End of, lass, no exceptions. Now fuck off out there and keep an eye on the patch. It'll be yours before you know it."

– Lenny Grafton, leader of the Barrington

Dear Diary

I'm young, too young some people would say, to take over the Barrington. What they don't understand is I've had years to learn the ropes, and Dad's always told me how to act when I'm in charge so I get the best out of people. So I get what I want— what he wants. While he's right, his advice mint, he hasn't factored in my true feelings. They don't matter,

3

he'd said. I have to hide them at all costs. If anyone sees my 'soft underbelly', I may as well give up.

On the outside, I'm everything he wants me to be, a woman who can step up to the plate and force people to do shit, but on the inside, sometimes I still have doubts, fears, insecurities that settle in my mind, deep-rooted weeds that'd grow wild if I gave them the chance. They whisper that I'm not good enough, I'll never get respect like Dad, so in order to run the patch without hassle, I'll have to bury a part of myself, the part with empathy, sympathy, and pretend that side of Cassie Grafton no longer exists.

Those who've known me all my life will be aware of the girl I really am, the one before I had to work for Dad once he got ill. They'll have thought I'm too weak to handle everything, yet for the few months I've taken on the main role, they've realised I'm a chameleon.

I've morphed into a hard little cow to prove myself so Dad knows his precious estate will be in good hands.

People will end up hating me, not understanding how I've changed so much from the happy, smiling woman of old into this...this monster who takes no nonsense.

I don't even like who I've become, but it's not an option to rule the Barrington as a soft-arse, much as I'd prefer to be lenient in some quarters, to relax the rules. Instead, when the day comes where Dad is gone and I'm fully in charge, I'll create new rules, as per his instructions, letting everyone know who's boss.

For the rest of my life, I'll be the new version of myself, the one who's hated but hopefully respected all the same, and I won't allow anyone to see the old me again.

Unless they've earnt that right.

I'm a bitch now, and that's something everyone needs to get used to.

Including me.

Chapter One

The Barrington Life – Your Weekly

GIRL MISSING, KIDNAPPED FROM MEAT FACTORY!

Karen Scholes – All Things Crime in our Time
Sharon Barnett – Chief Editor

SPECIAL EDITION – SATURDAY JUNE 28th 1997

Three-year-old Jessica Wilson, of the Barrington estate, was taken from Grafton's Meat Factory yesterday at four o'clock. She was there with her dad, Joe, who'd gone to pick up his wages after he'd handed in his notice so he can run Handel Farm. Someone took her. Literally took her. He had dark clothes on, a balaclava, and sped off in a small white van.

We at *The Barrington Life* can't get over it. She's one of our own, for fuck's sake, and we need to help find her. Don't forget that family has lived on our estate until moving to the farm last week. We stick together, we watch out for each other.

The police are searching, so they say, but we all know what they think of us lot, don't we. Scum, trouble, not worth bothering over. Well, Jessica isn't scum, and she *is* worth bothering over. We've sent this flyer out before our usual weekly because it's all hands on deck. Look in your sheds and garages, go out and walk the fields surrounding the meat factory in case she

8

was dumped. Check hedgerows, ditches, everywhere you can think of where someone would hide a little girl. Listen to conversations, because someone, somewhere, knows where that kiddie is, and we need to find her and take her home.

Any news, ring me or Sharon Barnett, or nip round to ours. If we're out, we'll have our mobiles. We'll find Jessica by ourselves. We don't need no coppers.

Lenny Grafton appreciated what those on the Barrington were doing, coming together like this. He'd been brought up on the estate from birth, owned the patch, and they had the same mind as him —and any who didn't, he soon twisted their arm into complying. They'd all band together and find the kid while he'd find the abductor. He didn't stand for nonsense on his turf, and justice would be served. You didn't just take a fucking lass, did you, especially not from outside his meat factory.

Don't step on Grafton turf, that was one of the terms, yet someone had done just that, breaking one of the golden rules. Two people, to be exact.

Whoever had snatched Jess knew she'd be there, and that concerned Lenny. They must have been watching the factory, maybe even worked there, or was it in the pub, them listening in when Joe had said on the phone he'd be back to collect his wages, and yes, he'd bring Jess with him for a visit.

A sadistic wanker. Once Lenny got his hands on him...

Sick, whoever had done it.

The weather had been shite all week, raining. June had been a washout. Wimbledon, cricket, and Glastonbury all ruined, everyone grumbling about it. Well, Joe's and Lou's lives were ruined at the minute, not to mention Jess's, and that was more important than people not being able to hang their washing out. The poor little girl must be shitting bricks being with strangers. He couldn't imagine the fear, the confusion at being separated from her mam and dad. Three years old, just like his Cassie. It didn't bear thinking about.

But the weather was a bonus in this case. The van's tyres had left tracks in the wet mud, so that was something Old Bill could chase up, plus there were several footprints where the van had been parked. Size nines so the copper had estimated, likely the treads of boots, and the fella had a navy boilersuit on. Maybe the police would look into that.

Joe had seen him take his child, watched helplessly as he'd threatened him with a shotgun and bundled Jess towards the back of the van where leather-gloved hands had come out and grabbed her, pulling her inside. Brown, that leather was, the attached arms hairy. Joe had moved to stand in front of the van to stop the driver leaving, but whoever it was had shot the vehicle forward, Joe ending up on the bonnet then

11

falling off onto the soggy ground. The van had sped away with the child in it, and Lenny's guts had gone south, his blood seeming to freeze. Who the fuck had the balls to nick a kid off of his property? Someone who didn't care for the consequences, that was who, a prick who didn't mind being dead when Lenny found him.

Did they think he was joking when he'd told them all his rules?

Dreadful. If anyone dared try that with Cassie, there'd be fucking hell to pay. Thank fuck he'd told his wife, Francis, to stop work at the factory near the end of her pregnancy and watch their kid. Then again, no one expected their child to be taken, did they, it always happened to someone else, and you felt for the parents on the telly, the appeal for the return of their precious person ripping your bloody heart out. Then you imagined how you'd feel and clutch your kid tight, praying it never happened to you.

Joe and Lou Wilson had become 'someone else', and maybe they'd opt to sit behind a long table with coppers and plead to the public to do the right thing if they'd seen something off. Lenny planned to find Jess before it got to that, though, but in the meantime, Joe and Lou would be inconsolable.

Why had they taken Jess, though, that was what got to Lenny. What did grown men need kids for if not the obvious—fiddling or for ransom? That sex trafficking shit had been going on a lot lately—he'd gone off his rocker when he'd found out some bloke kept women in his house on the Barrington, selling them off to dodgy punters—so had she been abducted for that reason? Were there men out there waiting for their order of a little girl? Or childless couples wanting a kid to call their own, buying her from a snatch-and-grab fake adoption agency?

He couldn't stand the thought of the former. Those types had rancid brains and hearts, weren't right in the head.

The Barrington Life *flyer fell from his hand onto the desk in his home office, previously a small dining room in their little two-bed home. Some daring bastard had crossed a massive line, and Lenny would find out who he was and shoot the fucker dead. Whoever had been in the back of that van would get it an' all.*

He left the room to find his missus. Francis would calm him down, get him to see sense through the red mist currently taking over. She was his rudder, the only one who could settle him, and he needed a clear head for this. Certain emotions had to be pushed aside so he could concentrate on finding the lass. He'd harden his heart, close his mind off from the horrors Jess could be going through, and seek out the targets.

She stood in the kitchen, his Francis, all five-foot-nowt beauty, her dark-dyed hair in a neat bun, her

14

posh clothes covered by an apron. She dyed that hair of hers from the original rich auburn, something their Cass had inherited. Francis had been bullied as a girl, called ginger nut and all sorts, so in her eyes, going darker meant she'd erased the cruelness thrown her way. She never had told him who'd picked on her. Probably a good move on her part because he'd have fucking killed them. She was one of his original sidekicks, sharing his desire to run the estate, and she knew as much as she needed to. He'd promised to tell her every little thing, but some shit he'd kept to himself. No point in her being upset, was there.

Cakes, she was making cakes with their Cassie, and he knew, just fucking knew she was doing it to remind herself how lucky she was it wasn't their child who'd been nabbed, taking time out to spend it with her, grateful she was there and not in some shithole with a bloke in a balaclava. Maybe she'd also thought about what Lenny had told her when she'd got pregnant: "That's it, Francis, you've got to step back, let me run things. You can't go gadding about in the middle of the night with me now. We can't risk you getting hurt."

Francis stopped smoothing the butter and sugar in the bowl, and Cassie stared across at him, an egg in each hand. Dodgy that, eggs in a three-year-old's mitts.

"What do you need?" Francis asked. As always, she'd sensed his silent request for help. She was a miracle, his wife.

"Clarity."

This was their code, the way they spoke around Cassie. He didn't want her knowing the proper bad side of their life until she grew up a bit. She wasn't old enough to understand the boiling rage that sent him out there with a gun or a knife, or his hands that were always ready to strangle people. She didn't need to understand it, not yet, but one day she'd run the estate, and she'd have to know all the ins and outs.

Not today, though.

"You stir this," Francis said to Cassie, taking away the eggs and popping them back in the carton. "Mammy won't be long."

Cassie took the spoon, her eyes alight, and Lenny would bet the little bugger dipped her hand in that bowl and ate some of the mixture. He glanced at Francis, giving her a look. She copped on straight away.

"No eating any of that," she said. "It's only sugar and butter, remember. You can lick the bowl when everything else has gone in."

"All right, Mammy." Cassie grinned, her tiny teeth on show, God love her.

Francis followed Lenny to his office and left the door ajar in case Cassie came a cropper. "Talk."

17

"I can't think straight," he admitted. "Can't see what's probably right in front of me. All I see is that kid being dragged into the van—and I was too far back in the bastard hallway at the factory to get there fast enough, to pick up my own gun. He'd driven off by the time I got out into the yard."

Lenny had jumped in his own van and given chase, but the wanker had disappeared in the maze of streets on the Barrington. A resident then, to know all the roads like that.

"Not your fault. I said that last night. Okay…" Francis let out a sigh and paced, a finger across her chin. "You said they must have known Jess would be there. You're in a rage, can't deal with owt but wanting to kill whoever it was, so you won't have checked who wasn't at work yesterday, would you."

The penny dropped, as it always did when Francis used her noggin. See? A rudder.

Lenny nodded. "So someone who works there, they had the day off to grab the kid?"

"Maybe. But they could also have got someone else to do it so they were at work and it didn't look suspicious — you know how this works, Len. People use others so they can stay in the background. You do it all the time. Who was around when Joe said he'd be coming for his wages?"

Lenny cast his mind back. There had been a couple of men within earshot when he'd asked Joe to bring Jess with him. She was a regular around their place, played with Cassie, and with the Wilson family moving off the Barrington to Handel Farm, Joe inheriting it from his old man who'd carked it recently, Lenny wanted to give her a present since they wouldn't be seeing her as much. Farm life was hard, and there were God knew how many pigs to look after.

That present, a big beige teddy bear with black eyes, had been dropped on the mud during the snatch. It had fallen from her chubby hands, and Joe had said he'd never forget her crying, reaching for it, then reaching for him when he'd stepped forward, shotgun aimed at him or not, to claim his girl back.

"Right. I'm off to the factory," Lenny said. "You'd better get back to Cassie. She'll have done fuck knows what to that butter by now, and as for the eggs…" Joe's daughter popped into his mind again. "Jess is three. Like our Cass. What the fuck must Joe and Lou be going through?"

"You know what to do, Len." Francis moved to the door. "Find whoever took her." She paused, grasping the handle. "And fucking kill them."

Chapter Two

"**G**et down on your fucking knees and beg me not to kill you." Jason Shepherd stared at the useless piece of shite who'd dared to tread on his toes, on Lenny's toes. He'd always hated him, had waited for an excuse to do him over, and now it had come. "Go on, do it."

He waved his gun with added menace, incensed this bastard wasn't immediately complying. A two-bit ponce, that's what he was, selling drugs on Lenny's turf, the divvy prat. Who the hell had the balls to do that? Richie Prince, apparently.

The empty house they eyeballed each other in stank of mould and piss and a touch of ancient old ladies. Yellow wallpaper peeled from the tops of the lounge walls, once lovingly put up by the former resident, who by all accounts had left the house to Lenny Grafton, the gangster in this part of the north. It was used for killing, for threatening, for torture, a nice out-of-the-way place on the edge of town. Handy, that.

Illuminated beneath the bare hundred-watt bulb, Richie finally obeyed, smirking—like he had room to do that, although it was clear he had the audacity—and glared at Jason. Sweat coated his forehead in tiny beads, his black hair sodden at the roots, and that beard of his, it needed a trim. He resembled a bloody hobo.

"You're no one," Richie said. "You don't get to tell me what to do."

No one. Well, that'd soon change. Jason was on the road to becoming *someone*, and the taste he'd had recently by helping Cassie Grafton out had given him the need for more—more money, status, every-bloody-thing.

And he'd get it.

"See, that's the thing," he said. "I *am* someone, only you won't accept that, and I *do* get to tell you what to do, seeing as Lenny Grafton pays my wages and I'm holding a gun." Jason jabbed it towards him for good measure, getting his point across, loving the feel of it in his hand. There was nothing better than gripping a piece. He itched to use it, desperate to make his mark, to show Lenny he really was worth having around.

"There probably aren't even any bullets in it." Richie laughed, the sound raspy from too many Lambert and Butlers, the odd spliff or two. Phlegmy. He could do with a bath, too, the scutty git. The stench of dried sweat came off him, overlaid with the freshness of fear, not that you'd know he was afraid. His attitude…seemed he wasn't bothered by Jason or the gun at all. "Like, it's got to be a toy."

Jason fumed inside, the red-hot heat of fury waiting to boil over, waiting for his permission to let it run wild. He'd struggled with controlling his temper all his life on account of his father. That man would have gone apeshit if Jason had shown him how arsey he'd got him, and now he wasn't in his life anymore, he wished he'd kicked the shit out of him before he'd left. At least he'd have that incident to look back on, to make him feel better. Instead, he had stained memories and a vat of hatred constantly simmering.

Outwardly, he remained calm, creating a blank mask—no facial movement, no telltale tics. It didn't do to let people like Richie think they'd got to him. *Keep your feelings close to your chest until the last second*, that was what his mentor, Lenny, had said, and Jason had stuck to that. So far. The thing was, if Richie riled him further, Jason might lose the plot. Blow his fucking head off.

"Do you want to test that theory of yours, though?" Jason tightened his finger on the trigger. Another couple of millimetres, and the bullet would release, game over, you tosspot.

He needed to get this sorted as soon as, scaring Richie into doing what Lenny wanted. Jason was meeting Cassie later for a bevvy or two at The Doncaster Arms. She thought he fancied her, that he wanted them to become an item, which they would if he had his way, but to be honest, she wasn't his type. With Lenny on his last legs, she'd be the next to take over the patch, and Jason needed an in with her—a proper in. He had plans to rule it himself, and nowt was going to stop him, not even her. Or her mother.

Richie snorted, still playing the hardman, although there was something in his eyes now, something different, the mad glint of a man intent on living for the rush diminishing a bit. Jason reckoned the dickhead couldn't keep this up for much longer. It took effort to maintain a façade.

And I should know.

Richie sighed, not quite beaten but possibly tired of playing this game. "Look, I sold a few wraps on Salway Street, big bloody deal. You've got your fingers everywhere, which means there's sod all places for others to peddle from. Why do you need *all* of this town? Why can't Lenny share? He always was a greedy bastard."

Jason froze at the disrespect shown to Lenny. The man had watched out for Jason for years, giving him advice his father should have, ensuring Jason's self-confidence grew from the battered thing it had been to the magnificent beast it was now. He'd even given him a job at the meat factory once he'd left school, pulling him out recently to help Cassie on the estate, plus oversee the drugs side of things. Some would say Jason had a massive ego, loved himself, and Lenny's teachings had turned him into an unlikeable character. Like Jason gave a shit. He had dreams, goals, and would prove to the world he was someone to take note of.

He'd have to explain things to Richie. Seemed the prat didn't get the rules. Drugs must have addled his brain so much he'd forgotten them.

"Because he calls the shots, because that's the way it works, how it's always worked since Lenny took over, and because I want money— lots of it. People already fear me since I took up working his patch, and it's addictive, watching them shit themselves. I'd say you should try it sometime, but that'd go against the rules, go against what you're allowed to do around here, and selling gear isn't one of them, not without Lenny's permission." He wafted the gun again, the weight of it well handsome, giving him courage. "Like I said earlier, beg me not to kill you."

"You can fuck right off on that one." Richie's face scrunched up, his brown irises obscured by almost-closed eyelids, the lashes thick like some woman. "I know you of old, remember, and you were a prick when we were kids, so why the hell should I do as you tell me since you're still a prick now?"

Don't let that get to you. Don't let him crawl under your skin.

Jason stifled the urge to kill him, this second. He'd killed before. His first victory had been in a fight, literally kicking someone's head in, his steel toecaps doing most of the work. He'd enjoyed it, no question, and having Lenny behind him meant he'd been shielded from any police involvement. Sorting Richie wouldn't stain Jason's conscience, he wouldn't give it a second thought, plus it'd stand him in good stead once

Lenny found out. He'd get a pat on the back, and the old fart may well reiterate to Cassie that Jason *was* someone to have on her side when she took control of the business; if Jason had his way, she'd only run it for a bit before he swiped it from under her nose, and she'd be in no position to do anything about it. Lenny might encourage them to be a couple, help things along a bit on that score. Jason had been working on her for months, but she was stubborn and hadn't taken the bait. What was all that about? Why didn't she want a bloke in her life yet?

"A prick, eh?" Jason swallowed. "Now then, that's not a nice thing to say."

"Yeah, well, I reckon—"

The bullet entered Richie's forehead, his eyes widening along with his rude-as-fuck mouth, one that wouldn't spew hateful words anymore. Brain matter and blood sprayed the rear wall, adding a fetching hue to the crappy wallpaper, red on banana-yellow, Pollock on acid. Richie fell backwards, his head cracking on the floor, the manky carpet beneath him a dull beige that might once have been dove-grey. With his calves tucked beneath him his pelvis tipped upwards, and Jason resisted stamping on the drug runner's nuts, just because he could.

Debris surrounded Richie, the sort of shit left behind when someone moved out, speckles of white and brown—the dried filth from shoe treads, bobbles of polystyrene, all manner of things that told stories about whoever had lived here. Some old bird, Jason had heard, who owed Lenny for helping her out back in the day. Probably why the place had strains of lavender in the air. All old biddies used that perfume, didn't they?

Claret seeped from the corner of Richie's mouth, trailing in a tributary along the bottom of his cheek and to his ear, pooling in the shell, a viscous red puddle. Jason moved closer to get a better look, his heart pumping, pulse thudding, adrenaline going mental. He admired his handiwork, puffing out his chest at the accomplishment. Yeah, notoriety was addictive, and shooting someone could be, too, if he let it take hold of him. Which he might. It beat administering a kicking. Quicker an' all, although messier.

The gun was nicked, couldn't be traced back to him. Lenny had given it to him as well as a stash of bullets, ordering him to use it with discretion. Well, Jason had done that, meeting Richie at the lone house on the outskirts. All the locals thought of it as 'the squat', what with its garden a riot of weeds and long grass to give that impression.

He'd parked his car around the back out of sight. Richie had turned up on a fucking bicycle of all things, one of those efforts with a motor or whatever, and Jason would have to flog it to some unsuspecting pleb. It folded up so would fit in the back seat, no problem. He'd get about fifty quid for it, seeing as it was hot. Better than a kick in the teeth.

Or a bullet to the head.

"Who's the prick now?" he muttered, then laughed, a full-on belly one, chuffed at himself something chronic. Who said crime didn't pay?

It paid dividends in boosting his ego.

Richie's eyes showed none of the earlier bravado. Vacant they were, staring at nowt, seeing nowt. Jason looked forward to the aftermath, giving his condolences to Richie's mother, Doreen, who happened to live a couple of doors away from him on the Barrington estate. That was the thing in their area, people got in with the wrong crowds, they all knew one another, and it was unlikely anyone managed to get out of that way of life completely. They were all connected in some way by Lenny, even those who had normal jobs. Everyone liked something that had fallen off the back of a lorry, didn't they. Richie was bound to go down the route he had, same as Jason with Lenny's encouragement, the rough element luring them in, whispering that they'd make a lot of cash if they went over to the dark side.

Jason wasn't as dark as he'd like to be, but one day, he'd be the fucking darkest. He'd live in Lenny Grafton's big gaff and lord it over everyone, Cassie by his side, maybe add a few nippers into the mix to keep her to heel. It'd be easy to fake love, to pretend—after all, he'd been pretending all his life, making out his father hadn't corrupted him, so no biggie. He'd rule, he'd call the shots, and no one would take it away from him. The power. The prestige. He'd chip away at Cassie bit by bit until she caved and let him rule the roost.

Her life.

He sighed. It was all very well dreaming, thinking of the future, but in the present, he had a body to get rid of. Richie was a scrawny fucker, no beef to him at all—all those drugs and barely any food—and Jason easily dragged him to his car. Darkness shrouded them, the light from the moon struggling to penetrate the black-bellied clouds, and the broccoli-shaped hedges bordering the main road further kept them invisible. No housing estate butted onto the back of the property, so unless some weirdo farmer traipsed his fields in the dark, Jason's antics wouldn't be seen.

He dumped Richie on the ground, loving the thud it created, the sense of power rushing through him that he'd killed this man, shut him up for good. He opened the boot, shifting a few things out of the way. A torch, a carrier bag containing more carrier bags, and a random spanner he'd used to fix Mam's pipe under her sink. He still lived with her, couldn't seem to leave, needing to look after her, show her his father had been a wrong 'un to treat her the way he had, that not all men were wankers. She had no clue about this other side of him. Although she knew he worked for Lenny, she wasn't aware of what he did. She thought he was a good boy, and no one could tell her any different.

Mam was the only woman he'd ever love like that.

He fished one of the bags out and, in the light coming from the boot, covered Richie's head with it, tying the handles beneath his chin. It wasn't because he couldn't stand looking at him, that seeing his face brought on a shedload of guilt, it was something else, something more practical, and nothing whatsoever to do with emotions. While he wasn't bothered about DNA transference—there was a fella who valeted for Lenny and kept his gob shut—he didn't much enjoy lumps of brain and shit messing up his boot carpet.

Jason parted his legs and bent them at the knees, then reached down to heft Richie into his arms. The man was all skin and bones, probably hadn't had a decent meal for years, Doreen telling him never to darken her door if he was 'running them bloody drugs'. Richie had stolen from her over the years, selling the stuff to fund his drug habit, and she'd finally had enough. Jason's mam would never disown him like that, she'd said as much.

"No matter what you do, you'll always be loved by me." That was what she'd said the day his father hadn't come home. "We'll stick together until the end."

Jason planned to prove that statement true, no matter what it took. He'd get her out of the little house he'd grown up in, one he hated with a passion (it was situated in the scabbiest street on the Barrington), and set her up somewhere nice. No way would he end up like Richie, who lived in a skanky bedsit—or he *had* lived in one—and Jason had a mind to nip over there after he'd seen Cassie to ransack it. There'd be a few baggies, he reckoned, full of weed, plus some of the white stuff, gear he could keep for himself. Apparently,

Richie stored it in one of those safes you get from Argos, told anyone who'd listen, too.

What an amateur.

"*You're* the prick, not me." Jason didn't need to wonder why that word was bothering him so much, the prick thing. His dad had called him that on the regular as far back as he could remember, and Richie saying it had lanced a ragged nerve.

He stuffed him in the boot, arranging his legs, placing his arms into whatever position meant he could fit him in—the boot wasn't that big. The bag of carriers rustled behind Richie's head, and for a moment, Jason thought someone was fucking about by the hedges out the front, then he reminded himself this place was out in the sticks, and he'd have heard a car, or the rustle of footsteps in the grass would have alerted him that someone was coming.

Jitters, they still got to him every now and then, not that he'd admit it to anyone.

He shut Richie in and walked down the side of the house, folding the bike into a compact shape that sat nicely in the back seat, cheers very much. A burst of cold December wind swirled, and if he were the fanciful sort, he'd imagine it was a portent, a warning of some kind, but he wasn't, so that idea went out of the window.

Back in the squat, he found a bucket, a scrubbing brush, and a smidgen of Fairy left in a bottle, green, the original sort, none of that pomegranate and jasmine shite. The place had hot water, so he filled the bucket, squirting washing-up liquid into the steaming flow, staring at the steadily rising bubbles. They reminded him of baths as a kid, of happier days when everything was so much easier—*if* Dad wasn't around. Jason had loved it just being him and Mam in the passages of time when Dad was away for work, but those passages always seemed more like specks, Dad home all too soon, gobbing off, slapping his wife, telling Jason he was a little prick.

"Fuck that," he mumbled and got on with cleaning up the wall in the living room. While Lenny had a crew who came and magicked away any evidence, there was no telling how quickly they'd get here. Best to attempt removing some of it before it dried, got caked on. Lenny would be proud of him for that.

The grubby carpet proved stubborn, the fibres holding on to the blood no matter how much Jason scrubbed at it. It ended up as a pink stain in the shape of Italy, fitting, what with the Mafia ties. Jason aspired to be at that level, so feared people worried he'd place a horse's head on their pillow. He'd have a think on that, come up with something else he'd be known for. Maybe the hearts of people he offed. Or toes. Something sinister like that.

He emptied the bucket, poking bits of brain down the plughole, and used bleach to wash the sink, careful not to splash it on his fancy suit jacket. Having done all he could, he left the house and drove towards town, then veered off on a track, heading for Grafton's Meat Factory. Lenny owned it, his front for a legitimate business, and two cousins would grind Richie up before the morning, feeding his minced body to the pigs up on Handel Farm.

He left Richie round the back beneath the usual tarpaulin behind the wheelie bins, securing it with blocks of concrete at the edges. The moon had won the fight with the clouds and shone brightly, enough for him to see what he was doing. He stared at the hump the corpse made, not that big to be fair, and imagined, if Richie was left to rot, what he'd look like in a few days. Foxes roamed these parts, and maybe they'd discover him and have a feast.

He chuckled and walked away, stopping short at the rumble of an engine. Breath held, he waited down the side of the building for a car to go past in the near distance, its headlights spearing cones into the darkness, the driver a murky silhouette, oblivious that a body lay close by, that Jason stood watching, a dark blot against the sooty bricks. This sort of shit fired him up more than owt else, him knowing, others unaware, crime being played out while they lived their usual boring lives.

The car moved on, and he stared at the taillights until they were red pinpricks in the gloom. He got in his Fiesta and sniffed. Bleach on his skin. Bugger it, he'd have to go home and change, shower before meeting Cassie. But first, he had to message Lenny, report back, telling him there was one less interloper to worry about.

He smiled, anticipating the congratulations.

Chapter Three

The Doncaster Arms on the Barrington estate, known as The Donny to locals, was packed to the gills, the air laden with the heat of so many close bodies and the smells they produced. Cassie had been coming here all her life, her first visit in a buggy at three weeks old, everyone cooing over her, apparently. Dad had been so proud, so he kept telling her, and more often than not lately, he slipped into the past whenever she popped into his office at his and Mam's place to see him. She lived in a flat above their garage but had taken to sleeping in the family home when Dad's heart started played him up.

Recently, he'd told her the end was near, he could feel it calling to him, whispers in the night while he stared at the ceiling, Mam asleep beside him. That had scared the shit out of Cassie, not only because she couldn't imagine life without him and his steady influence, but she'd have to take over the estate, become the person he'd been priming her to be, someone without sentimental feelings, the thorn in people's sides.

He loved talking about the old days, though, focusing on them more than the present. That was a bit of a problem, considering he had to get everything in order before he...before he died, but she didn't have the heart to cut him off mid-sentence. It was strange to see her father this way, reminiscing, smiling at his past antics, as if he wanted to remember his time as the leader from the start until now, relive it all inside his head, bringing it alive to Cassie with his words. It tired him out, and Mam usually came in and told him off for it.

She hated thinking about his decline so switched her attention to her surroundings. The bottle-blonde Doreen Prince sipped a gin and tonic at the bar with her lover, Harry Benson, his bony arm going up and down as if he couldn't get the booze inside him quickly enough, a pale ale clutched in a pint glass.

Most of the neighbours from Cassie's old street were in for a Friday night knees-up, although there weren't many knees going anywhere at the minute. Come ten o'clock, though, and everyone would be pissed as farts and the fun would kick off. The landlord, Geoff Davis, was setting up the karaoke, and the rest of the evening promised punters strangling the hell out of songs while Cassie tried not to wince.

She leant back in the booth and watched the door. Jason was late, unusual for him, and she worried he'd got caught up in business. Everyone who grafted for her father had smartphone burners they used for work, but hers hadn't gone off with a message alert. She dug around in her bag, her fingers breezing over tampons, a lipstick, and what felt like an ancient Mars she'd bought ages ago and had forgotten about. She checked the mobile, then dropped it back inside. A glance at her personal one showed no text there either, so she shrugged and swallowed a mouthful of vodka and tonic.

Geoff spouted his usual, guffing on into the microphone about people putting their names forward to sing—"Fill out the slip, and let's get this party started!"—and Cassie tuned him out, preferring to listen to the conversation filtering through the banister-like rails that separated her booth from the one beside it. Trevor Bayliss and his wife, Lisa, worked for Cassie's dad and shouldn't be discussing business in public. She'd hate to have to poke her head through two rails and warn them, but if they didn't shut up, she'd have to. She was working in Dad's place now, and if she let this violation slide, people would think she was a soft touch.

"So she hasn't let you know owt yet then?" Lisa sounded disinterested, likely wanting to shove work aside on their night out but knowing she couldn't. Grafton work was twenty-four-seven, no bones about it. "Hasn't she even contacted Lenny or Cassie?"

"No, and Lenny will be gunning for her. She was supposed to report back to me hours ago, you know how it goes. I get a bit sick of her acting like she has her own set of rules. She could fuck things up by breaking them." Trevor cleared his throat.

"What if something's happened to her and she *can't* report back?" Lisa was worried now, that much was obvious.

"Fuck, I didn't think of that."

Lisa huffed out a snap of breath. "No, you wouldn't, because you're not a woman who has to worry about being alone with men. Bloody stupid idea this scheme is, if you ask me, *and* her going without someone covering her arse chaps mine. She's with those blokes, and any one of them could take a funny turn and lash out at her."

Cassie searched her brain for what job they were talking about. It sounded like it might be one of the sex workers, but as far as she was aware, none of them had a specific job—unless Dad had actioned something and hadn't told her. No, he wouldn't do that. He was still sharp with regards to work, his brain unaffected by his dodgy ticker. He was staying off the patch a lot while he waited for an op to fix it, Mam insisting he take it easy—or easier, seeing as he still wanted updates from Cassie every night and dished out orders for her to carry out. Even the stress of that couldn't be good for him.

It had to be the job Brenda Nolan was on, getting her hooks into some bloke on his last legs, ensuring he left his money to her. Dad had a contact at the hospital who passed on the names of people who were likely to snuff it, those with a fair bit of dosh, and Brenda posed as a home carer, doing their housework and whatnot while wheedling her way into their affections *and* their beds. Not something Cassie enjoyed knowing about, but it was hard not to pick up on things when she lived with her old man. His voice carried, seeping out of his office and into the living room or kitchen when he had meetings. Besides, she'd read all his ledgers so knew everything that went on.

Didn't mean she had to like it. Maybe, when she ruled the estate, she'd scrap the scamming old men side of it. She didn't know what Dad was thinking, doing shit like that, and as for Mam agreeing with him…

"So she went to his house, yes?" Lisa asked.

"Yeah, and hasn't been heard of since."

"When did she go?"

"I don't know, but she was supposed to report in about five."

Lisa sighed. "For God's sake, that's not long ago. She's probably got her burner switched off. Look, you ought to ring Lenny and let him know, and if he agrees, we can go round to the bloke's house, see if she's okay."

Ring Lenny? For fuck's sake.

Cassie had heard enough. Everyone had been told not to bother Dad and to deal with her, and their blatant disregard for her being in charge pissed her off. She got up on her knees and stared through the rails, gripping two in tight fists. "Keep your fucking voices down, will you?"

Trevor blanched, his white skin pale against his black hair, dyed to cover the grey. His caterpillar eyebrows met in the middle, and his mouth gaped. "Shit, didn't see you there."

"No," Cassie said, "and I could have been anyone. You *know* you're not to talk about work in public. Some people around here will listen in and pass the info on to whoever and cause trouble."

Twin spots of colour infused Lisa's cheeks. She ran a hand through her short blonde hair (Annie Lennox, anyone?) and glared at her husband, as if to tell Cassie it was his fault. "How much did you hear?"

"Enough for me to tell you to go to the man's place and check on Brenda. I'll let the gossiping slide this time, but if I ever find out you've done it again, you'll know about it. Message me once you know she's okay—Dad's had a bad turn this evening, and I don't want you bothering him.

Plus, *I'm* the boss at the minute, so it's me you report to. Leave him alone."

Trevor looked as if he wanted to protest, puffing his chest out, but Cassie stared him out until he dipped his head. She'd be taking over for good one day, and Trevor needed to know she was as strict as her father and wouldn't take any shit. Sod that she was a woman, she could run things just as well. Her dreams of university had been dashed once Dad's prognosis had been revealed a few years ago, so if she couldn't be a teacher, she'd bloody well be a gangster. Why not? She knew how it worked. Dad had taught her everything: how to behave, how to control her emotions, how to deal with prats like Trevor who probably hated having to answer to her. How to shut these two up if they continued to flout the rules.

"Right," Trevor said, suitably meek, although defiance still lingered in the tightening of his features, his crow's feet bunching. It probably killed him to obey her.

He took Lisa's hand and guided her out of their booth, his cheeks flushed and his jaw set, every movement jagged, giving away what was going through his head. She'd humiliated him, but that was tough shit.

They weaved through the customers amid the strains of *Unchained Melody* sung by Doreen's Harry, and Cassie released a long breath then sucked in another, coaching herself to remain calm. She'd have to get used to dishing out orders, being mean to people. It went against her usual kind nature, but what else could she do? If people got a whiff of her being a softie when it came to Barrington business, they'd stamp her underfoot, and everything would turn to shit.

Cassie couldn't allow her father's hard work to be ruined because of her.

She was younger than Trevor and Lisa by a couple of decades, and they probably viewed her as some stupid kid, but she'd grown up listening to her father, knew the business off by heart, and wouldn't stand for any nonsense. She'd keep her true emotions inside no matter how much she disliked herself for being a hard-nosed bitch.

She was a Grafton and would be treated as such, and those who balked at that, well, they could go and do one. Dad expected no less, and she'd have to learn to be the same way.

She downed her drink and walked to the bar, leaving her bag and coat in the booth. No one would dare take them. She squeezed between two old men she'd known all her life, cousins who ran the butcher's stall on the Saturday market, but their main job during the week was at the meat factory. Felix and Ted Smith had often given her pocket money in her childhood, sometimes a bag of sweets if she went past their stall with Mam, and she'd seen them as kindly fellas who'd moved here from Yorkshire, no wives or children of their own. Now, they were still kindly, but they had a sinister side, disposing of bodies left out the back of the factory then taking them to Handel Farm for the pigs to trough on.

The things she'd heard throughout her lifetime... She ought to be disgusted, and if she were anyone else, she would be, but the life of a gangster was ingrained in her, and getting things done when no one else would do it was a part of that life. Granted, some people got killed, some maimed, and some plain disappeared, but it was the way, the rules here, and she'd live by them the same as everyone else.

Those who didn't? They were dealt with.

She'd hide her disgust and sorrow, stuffing it deep down so she never had to feel it. When she'd known she'd have to take over sooner than she'd thought, she'd created what she thought of as her 'monster', a new person, one who could handle all the horror, so far removed from the young girl she'd been, the one before Dad had told her what he really did to make money. She'd had an idea, though. The kids at school had whispered his name, fearful of him, so she'd known something was up. From the day he'd explained, the monster had been born, growing bigger and bigger over the years into the bitch it was now.

"Ah, there she is, our Cassie." Felix grinned, his dentures slipping.

"How's it going?" she asked.

"Same old, same old."

Ted slurped some beer. "How's Lenny?"

Cassie was used to people asking that these days. She wondered if they were genuine queries half the time or whether people were gauging how long it would be before she took the reins properly. A few would love to see her fail so they could throw it in her face that as a woman, she wasn't up to the job. If only Lenny had a son, that sort of bollocks. But she'd show them and, dare she even think it, she'd be *better* than her father. She had Mam to protect, Mam to think about. Anyone who got in the way of caring for her once Dad died would see a gun pointed at their fucking face.

"He's tired this evening, had a bit of a turn," she said. "Staying in tonight. Mam ordered a Chinese and told him to put his feet up."

"I could do with one of those." Felix nodded at Ted, his grey hair a cloud. "You up for that?"

Ted finished his drink. "I heard old Li Jun's got a special offer on. Two curries for the price of one."

Cassie loved the food from the Jade Garden and fancied a curry herself. She'd suggest it to Jason—*when* he finally got here. And there he was, conjured into being by her thoughts, muscling in through the dense crowd, his reflection in the mirror behind the bar showing he had a beef about something. She spun and smiled, although he didn't return it.

Shit had gone down.

She leant forward to whisper in his ear, "What's the matter?"

"Fucking Richie Prince. Your dad's aware—I sent a message. Your old dear replied, said to tell you." He rubbed his temples in circles, looking at Felix and Ted, saying to them, "There's a job waiting for you."

Felix cuffed his nose, his coat sleeve earning a wet stripe. "Bollocks. That's the Chinese dinner up the swanny."

"Can't it wait until morning? There's a spring roll calling my name." Ted tugged at his earlobe.

"Tomorrow's Saturday, you prat," Felix said. "We do the market, don't we."

"Chuffing hell." Ted sighed. "Come on then."

They walked away, and Jason took Ted's spot. Cassie stared ahead into the mirror, watching for anyone else listening, especially Doreen Prince. It was best they didn't talk here, Cassie couldn't be doing with earwiggers, and she ought to practise what she preached. Trevor and Lisa had already been reprimanded for nattering too loudly.

"Let's nip to the Jade Garden," she said.

Cassie scooted to the booth, now filled with other people's arses, and collected her handbag and thick jacket. She gave them a filthy look for taking her seat without asking, moving her stuff to the edge so they had room. They appeared chastised, so she left it at that.

"Pick your battles, Cass," Dad had once said.

Jason waited for her by the door, opening it for her, letting in a blast of freezing air. She shrugged her coat on, zipped it up, and stepped outside, the chill cooling her heated cheeks. Bag strap in a diagonal across her chest, she tamped down her annoyance at Jason sending Dad a message when he *knew* he had to go through her. Jason had a habit of taking matters into his own hands, and it annoyed her.

They walked side by side, heads bent against the brisk wind, and Cassie told him to dish the gossip.

His story wasn't unusual, no different to many others she'd heard, but the fact he'd killed Richie pissed her off so much she wanted to slap him. Jason was supposed to beat him up at the squat, not fucking murder him, and while the body and evidence would be long gone soon, that wasn't the point. Richie, a tad on the dickhead side, would have been a good person to have in her corner. A grass, managing to get information by loitering the way he did—walls had ears, but Richie also had a mouth to pass his findings on to her. Or he had at one time.

She took her burner phone out and fired off a quick message to the cleaning crew, then turned her attention back to Jason, placing her mobile in her bag. "Why shoot him?" She lifted her head to check for passersby also on their way to the Chinese. Hands stuffed in pockets in lieu of gloves, she muttered, "What a fucking stupid thing to do. He was supposed to get another warning."

"He got my goat, pushed it. I did what your old man told me to and used discretion. I made the decision, end of. Can't change it now, can we. He'll be mince within the hour, so what's the problem?"

Cassie thought of Doreen smiling at Harry while he'd bodged up that song on the karaoke, how that smile would be wiped away soon. Despite her casting her son out of the family home, she must still love him. Feelings didn't just stop, did they.

Dad never let anyone's death go unannounced. If he didn't want people to know it was to do with him, he sent anonymous notes so at least folks could have a wake or whatever. All right, they didn't usually have bodies to bury, but knowing they were dead went some way to helping the grieving process. *Not* knowing was what killed you inside, the wondering, the endless questions with no answers. Other times he got Karen Scholes and Sharon Barnett to put things in *The Barrington Life*, coppers unaware of what was really being said, residents knowing only too well because he'd told them all at one time or another what the hidden meanings meant.

"Why did he piss you off? Was it something more than the drugs?" She came to a stop outside the Jade and browsed the lit menu, hanging in the window, and waited for him to respond.

He wouldn't like answering to her, not when Dad was still alive, but like he'd been told, she was helping out, getting ready for her role, and Jason would have to deal with it whether he liked it or not. He had some weird sense that he was family because Dad had taken a shine to him, but he *wasn't* a Grafton, never would be, so she'd have to stop this nonsense where he took matters into his own hands.

He still had a lot to learn, and she wasn't sure he was up for it.

If they became a couple like he'd sort of suggested recently, how would it work at home in their private time? She was a strong woman, had a will of iron inherited from Lenny, and she doubted she'd back down from Jason in any aspect of their relationship. Could he handle that? Could he stand being second fiddle to a housing estate?

That was a discussion for another day, and she hadn't made up her mind whether she'd take him up on his offer anyroad. She'd run the business better on her own, no manly distractions.

"Didn't you hear me?" she snapped. "*Why* did he piss you off?"

The glow from the Chinese menu board played on his face, stark yellow, unnatural, like his liver was on the way out. "He called me a prick."

Is that all? "So?"

"I don't like it." Arcs of mustard-coloured light gave his cheekbones a sunken appearance, and his bottom lip stuck out.

God, he's such a child.

"Any particular reason?" The words 'Chop Suey' swam in her vision, tears of anger fuzzing things. She hated it when that happened. People probably mistook the tears for weakness.

Jason cleared his throat. "Not one I'm prepared to go into at the minute, no."

While she couldn't force him to give up his reasons, she boiled inside that no matter what the rules were, he was entitled to keep private stuff to himself—and she sensed it was private.

"Is it going to naff you off in the future? That could be a problem, especially with you being my current right hand." She had to make it clear from the get-go: if he was likely to become a liability, he could fuck off now. She didn't intend steering a sinking ship, and any hands who mucked up weren't welcome on her deck.

"No," he said. "Your mam said she's sending a crew to the squat."

"Why didn't you tell me that before I fucking messaged them?"

He smirked.

She didn't.

"And now I have to find another grass. Richie would have been decent at it." She sighed, her breath clouding in the cold air, rising to disappear at the top of the menu board. *I wish he'd disappear.*

Jason frowned. "Why you? It's not your full responsibility yet."

She rammed her hands on her hips, narked at him assuming shit. "And you know that *how*?"

He shrugged, nonchalant, like he didn't give a monkey's she was riled. "Lenny runs the patch."

"With me alongside him." She stiffened her spine, words of rebuke lining up on her tongue. Once again, though, she'd choose her battles and opted for a tamer approach. "D'you know, you can go off people, especially those who make it clear they can't follow rules. You *know* I'm his right hand now."

He seemed to flip off his arrogant mood and stared at her, gripping the tops of her arms, not too tightly, but enough to get his need across. Was he *panicking*? This was an emotion she didn't associate with him. He was like her monster, rarely showing his other side. So why reveal something now?

He shook his head. "I'm having a bad day, that's all. I've got no problem with you dishing out orders."

That was a swift turnaround. "Best you don't, or you know what'll happen." She left the threat hanging and brushed his hands off, walking into the Jade. The scents of fried rice, soy sauce, and char siu wafted at her, and she smiled at Li Jun behind the counter, his family working in the kitchen beyond, visible through a square opening in the wall. It seemed like she'd known them forever. She'd gone to the same school as his sons.

"Come for the package instead of me bringing it to you?" he asked, his white chef's jacket stained with curry sauce splashes, a pen for writing down the orders sticking out of the breast pocket. He was a short man, slender, and although he smiled a lot, sometimes he appeared sad, staring off, thinking.

"Yes, I can take it if you like, although I haven't got my car, so it's a bit risky. Hang on." She turned to look at Jason behind her. "Got yours close by?"

Jason's forehead ruffled. "Yeah, why?"

Christ, he was questioning her despite implying he wouldn't. Why did he always have to push things? Wind her up? It was like he enjoyed toying with her. Maybe, because he'd known her before she'd had to become hardened, he thought he could wear her down.

How wrong he was.

The hairs on the back of her neck twitched. "None of your pissing business why. Go and get it."

He scowled then schooled his features into a more reasonable expression—one that didn't tell her he despised having to obey her. Well, he'd have to get used to that, wouldn't he, because the new Cassie Grafton backed down for no one.

Chapter Four

The Barrington Life - Your Weekly

JESS STILL NOT FOUND! WHO THE HELL HAS
HER?

Karen Scholes - All Things Crime in our Time
Sharon Barnett - Chief Editor

Someone knows where she is. Why are you keeping the secret? How can you stand yourselves knowing Jess is hidden somewhere? How do you sleep at night? Are you keeping her safe? Fed? What the hell are you playing at?

Look, are you being threatened? You know what to do if you are. Contact Lenny Grafton or Glen Maddock, his right hand. They'll look after you. Or, if you know who's done this, don't sit there letting some bastard get away with it. You must know it's wrong.

We've got an update on Jess's clothing when she was taken. Pink leggings and wellies. A white T-shirt. Transparent coat, rainbows all over it. Apart from the coat, it's all the Ladybird brand from Woolies. She's blonde, curly hair, had it in a ponytail with one of them bobbles that has two plastic pink flowers on it, yellow balls in the middle. Have you seen a little girl like that since Friday 27th? Has someone suddenly appeared with a child they didn't have before, passing her off as their own?

Joe and Lou's farmhouse and pig barn have been searched by the police, plus the land. Can you believe that? Like they're guilty or something. Not them two, they wouldn't harm a hair on their kiddie's head. No, it's someone else. Two people. One bloke took her, the other was in the back of the van. As their identity wasn't seen, it could even be a woman. Think about that, a *woman* helping to steal a child.

As for that van, we have info. It's a B reg, an '84 plate, so they're not rolling in it with a new vehicle. Ford, small, white. Do you know anyone who owns one of those? Doesn't matter whether the plate isn't a B, they could have used false ones, the slimy gits. We need you. Talk to us. Let's get that girl back home where she belongs. We're a family on the Barrington, and no one messes with our babies.

Karen Scholes dropped the final flyer through the last letterbox and sighed with relief and frustration,

77

worn out from traipsing the streets. No one she'd spoken to today knew owt, and no one seemed dodgy. She prided herself in sniffing out a liar once the first few words came out of a fibber's gob, but everyone had been as concerned as she was, even the usual scallies. She'd disturbed many a Sunday dinner by knocking on doors and asking questions. Not one resident had minded—or they hadn't seemed to anyroad. All day it had taken her, but she had to do something. She couldn't sit at home while little Jess was with God knew who. Sharon Barnett was delivering to the other side of the Barrington along with some teens who went down the middle, paid a few quid for it.

Karen's kids were adults now, scuttling out of her coop as soon as they'd got a job, making their own way, each of them in one of the high-rise flats, rented off Lenny Grafton. She'd taught them never to succumb to Lenny's offers of work, and as far as she knew, neither of them had—they'd told her they didn't agree with working for a man like him, and she believed them. Lenny was a nice enough bloke if you were on the right side of him, but he wasn't the employer Karen wanted for her son and daughter.

She thought back to when they were small, how fear had gripped her if they wandered off in the supermarket or whatever. Her blood always ran so cold, her mind shorting out for a moment in panic, then a rush of bad situations filled it: men snatching them down the sweetie aisle; her kids trying to cry out behind the hands covering their mouths; their legs kicking as they struggled to breathe. Then she'd spotted them, and her body heated up, a rush of goosebumps showering her skin, her eyes filling with tears of relief.

"Get your arses here now! Don't you ever scare me like that again!" And she'd clipped them round the backs of their heads, looking as if she hadn't cared they'd vanished for an instant at all, yet she'd been terrified.

Lou must be feeling the same, except she was terrified little Jess wasn't coming home.

The idea of someone taking her babies… God, what must Lou and Joe be going through? Karen would go out of her mind. This was her only way to help, writing the extra flyer while also compiling the usual weekly pamphlet she organised with Sharon. Lenny provided the computers, printers, ink, and paper. He called her and Sharon his secretaries and left them in charge of informing residents of any news on his behalf.

It hadn't always been like that, though. Once upon a time, Karen and Sharon had all but run the estate. Until Lenny had stomped along in his size tens.

Karen and Sharon didn't have husbands, their useless men long gone, Karen's still around somewhere, she saw him on the estate from time to time, but Sharon's had left and never came back. They *worked together at Kwik Save during the week as a cover and supplemented their income by selling hooky gear for Lenny, plus writing the articles and informing him of any gossip. Yeah, they'd succumbed to his charms back in the day, Karen begrudgingly, although she'd pretended otherwise. Then her old man had left her for a woman with perkier tits and a barely legal age on her birth certificate, the paedo. What was she supposed to do with children to feed? Karen was sometimes stifled by Lenny's orders, what he asked her to do, hence why she hadn't wanted her kids to go down the same road. It was all right for her but not for them.*

She was more than stifled by him taking over what was once hers, but you didn't deny the man anything. He was a right hard bastard, and truth be told, he scared her sometimes, although she'd never admit that to anyone.

She sighed once more and pulled her hood up. It was threatening to bloody rain again. In June, you were meant to hang your washing out, weren't you, and sunbathe in the garden, a nice glass of chilled wine by your side. Not this year. It was nippy an' all, everything so gloomy.

It matched the mood of the estate. No one had much to smile about, not with Jess gone and suspicion around every corner.

She stared across at Sculptor's Field, the large patch of grass no one seemed to own, situated behind the last row of houses on the outskirts. Beyond it, fields stretched out, belonging to Joe Wilson, passed down to him by his father along with Handel Farm, although he didn't appear to be doing anything with the land.

The grass directly ahead had a weird thing in the middle, white stone, as tall as a lamppost, as wide as a shed, and folks in these parts reckoned that's where the name had come from. Some sculptor had fashioned a horse of sorts, or maybe it was a mythical being, which stood on a cement plinth mid-clop. Most days kids swung off the bent knee at the front while others hung off the tail, a curved-up protrusion out of the arse end.

Fucking odd thing. Everyone called it The Beast.

She'd walk along the edge of Sculptor's Field behind the Barrington and save herself a bit of time. If she went home via the streets she'd get stopped by someone asking questions, and she was too weary to answer them now. One of the women down her road, Brenda Nolan, her best friend, had saved her a roast dinner, and Karen looked forward to tucking in. She'd try not to think about whether Brenda had washed her hands or not before cooking. The woman worked for Lenny, touching old men—Karen didn't even want to go there.

She took a deep breath, stuffed her hands in her soggy coat pockets, and headed off. The Beast stood side-on, its tail pointing towards the estate, its nose raised to the overcast sky as if the horsey bastard sniffed the damp air coming in off Joe's land. The mane, crafted clumsily in her opinion, poked up in spikes, and she'd always worried children would climb up, slip, and get their eyes gouged out.

Karen thought a lot of things she shouldn't. Maybe it was the mother in her, seeing danger all around. Or maybe she was a tad sadistic.

Almost at the stone creature, she shuddered. It had always given her the creeps, especially as it had arrived overnight, some unseen stranger placing it there. They'd have needed a crane, and who the hell could that have been? There was nowt so queer as folk.

A fresh wave of tiredness came over her—she'd walked miles today, the Barrington a massive estate— so she sat on the end of the plinth, the tail above her, and contemplated life for a bit.

Only a bit, though, as her mind tended to wander to how she was a lonely cow with only Sharon and Brenda to keep her company in the evenings. Well, when Brenda wasn't off tending to the elderly fellas. Karen wasn't meant to know about that little scheme, but Brenda had confessed one night after Sharon had gone home. Drunk as anything, Brenda had spilt one too many beans from a can that also contained wriggling worms. She'd sworn Karen to secrecy. Ever since, images of what Brenda did in order to earn money for Lenny's coffers popped into Karen's mind from time to time, like now.

She shivered at the image of Brenda giving an old man one then pushed it out of her head. Stood. Stretched her back out, the bloody thing cracking. She might need to go and see a doctor about that.

Karen moved to plod on, taking a step past the side of the plinth. Something appeared in her peripheral, a light-coloured mass, and she reckoned someone had dumped a white bag of rubbish, the filthy fuckers. She turned to have a proper look, intending to pick it up and dispose of it properly in one of the public bins, but the sight that greeted her prevented that.

All the breath left her lungs.

It wasn't a white bag of rubbish.

Damp pink leggings grew out of small wellies. A rainbow-covered raincoat swaddled a chubby torso in a white T-shirt. A ponytail, blonde hair, the curls wet slugs. A hair bobble, the flowers she'd been told about, shiny from rain.

Jess Wilson.

"Oh God, oh my fucking God…"

Chapter Five

Brenda Nolan had a bit of a problem. A problem that would be Lenny's or Cassie's once she admitted what she'd done, but she didn't much fancy pissing Lenny off when he was poorly. He could be a grouchy bastard when well, so bugging him now? No, ta. Hours she'd been here, pondering this and that, waiting for night to fall so if someone had to come round, they were less likely to be seen. Everyone who lived in this street was old, so they'd probably go to bed early, but still, she didn't want to take the risk some elderly bugger had stayed up to watch the telly.

She'd known Lenny for years, worked for him, and he paid her a tidy sum every time she conned the dying, plus a weekly wage. She supposed what she did was distasteful, but when you'd grown up poor, wondering where your next meal was coming from, you tended to do anything to keep the wolf from the door. Well, she did. Her job was money for old rope, the easiest she'd ever earnt.

She remembered the hunger, the gripes in her belly, the weakness from lack of food, and never wanted to go back there again. All right, she could have worked in one of the three little shops on the estate, but blimey, with the gob she had on her, she'd scare customers away. She wasn't one for mincing her words, tending to give it to someone straight—no one got crossed wires then. Besides, she wouldn't earn enough to buy all the things she wanted if she stood behind a counter, her talent for lying to old men wasted. She'd got used to living the good life, too. Some might wonder why she still lived in the house she did, not moving to a bigger, nicer place, but she'd done it up over the years and didn't want to leave. It was home, and she was happy there with Karen just along the road.

She was good at what she did, extracting cash sums from men desperate to have one last shag or twenty before they carked it, a woman to love, who took care of them, played the role of wife without the wedding ring. She didn't much like wiping their arses when it came to *that* time, but needs must, and she put her head down and got on with it, her eye on the eventual prize. Some called it prostitution, she called it being entrepreneurial, and it *was* work, no matter what anyone said. Some nights she went home bloody knackered and flopped into bed, snoring in no time.

Michael Peg, the old boy she'd been buttering up, wasn't breathing. She'd been coming to see him for three months, every day without fail, dressed up to the nines, giving him something to lust after while his kidneys grew more diseased by the day. He'd questioned her clothing at first, wondering why she wasn't in some nurse's uniform or whatever, but she'd said being freelance meant she could wear what she liked.

He'd swallowed it, *and* the fake documents she'd produced that claimed she was a carer, NHS approved. She even had a lanyard.

"Blimey, what a pickle, Michael. I bet you didn't think that was the way you'd go out, did you? I know I bloody didn't."

She waited for an answer, hoping she was wrong and he wasn't dead, but he remained mute, his glassy eyes staring her way.

She checked his pulse again—nowt—and even put her ear to his mouth to see if any breath came out. He smelt of vinegar from the chips she'd fed him for lunch, and a bit of gravy from a steak and kidney Pukka pie had dried on his lips.

Nasty.

"I didn't expect you to have a ruddy heart attack, did I?" she said, brushing his hair into a tidier style. He was colder than the last time she'd touched him. How long did it take for that rigor mortis thing to kick in? When would he go all stiff, making it difficult to remove him from the house? Someone would have to break his bones to straighten him out, and she shuddered at the sound of it playing inside her head.

Hours ago, she'd gripped his hair while straddling him on the sofa, giving him what he'd wanted, the randy old dodger, staring at the wall and wondering whether to replace her fridge freezer with one of those big American efforts as the old one made a funny clonking sound. Halfway through the ride of Michael's life, he'd jolted. She'd assumed he'd got excited too quickly and had finished, but his eyes had bulged, foam coming out of his slack mouth, plus this weird noise, one cats let out when they were about to fight. She'd leapt off him and staggered away, her heart beating fast, her legs going weak, her sights on his deflated willy.

Eventually, she'd calmed down and washed him, tucked him away and zipped up his trousers, and sat on the armchair opposite, legs crossed, contemplating what to do. Usually, these men died of natural causes, and she supposed this *would* be classed as natural—death by shagging—but she was always at her house when they left this mortal coil, well away from the houses when they breathed their last, so she couldn't be blamed for owt.

The cash sat in a large padded yellow-beige envelope on the mantel, between an old black-and-white photo of Michael and his late wife on their wedding day and a duck ornament, complete with creepy feathers, so that wasn't a concern. She'd have been well upset if he hadn't withdrawn it yet, but he'd managed a trip to the bank in a taxi this morning, sprightlier than usual—maybe he was doing that rallying thing dying people did—so she'd get paid her portion of it. The thing was, should she take it?

Lenny usually chose men without families, but this one had a daughter who lived in Cornwall, and she'd likely query the withdrawal, seeing as it was probably her inheritance. Brenda had hoped more time would pass, the withdrawal far in the past enough that it wouldn't be poked into too much. All the other blokes had been lonely fellas, no one to call their own, and any money hadn't been flagged. Not that she was aware of anyroad. For all she knew, Lenny could have dealt with that. He knew so many people, ones who'd turn a blind eye to him asking them to cover shit up.

Brenda lit a cigarette and fished her phone out of her handbag, selecting Lenny's number. She really didn't want to phone him, seeing as he was poorly, but what else could she do? Maybe contact Cassie? This wasn't something she thought her handler needed to know about before the Graftons.

A knock at the front door startled the crap out of her, and she let out an "Ooh!" of surprise, slapping a hand over her mouth. No one came here other than her, Michael had told her that, not even delivery drivers (she bought his shopping), so maybe it was a canvasser or something. She stubbed her ciggie out in the flower-patterned saucer perched on the chair arm and rose, her legs a little wobbly. She rarely got spooked, but when she shared a room with a dead body, she was bound to be on edge. Michael watched her as she walked past the sofa, or it seemed like he did. What a strange man.

At the window, she stood to one side, pulled the edge of the burgundy velvet curtain back an inch, and peered across at the doorstep to the right. The black Victorian lamp attached to the house lit up Trevor and Lisa Bayliss, that nutty married couple, and she expelled a sigh of frustration. Trevor was her handler, and the less he knew about this fuck-up the better. As for him bringing his missus... What was he playing at?

Brenda rushed to the armchair and snatched up her work burner, tapping out a message: *Go away. All fine here.*

Back at the window, she nosed out. Trevor held his phone up and prodded the screen. Fab, he was responding to her, something else she didn't need.

Trevor: *What the fucking hell have you been up to all evening? You were meant to clock in by five.*

Brenda: *I got distracted. Michael wanted to play Scrabble.*

A lie, but Trevor wasn't to know that. She'd never played anything with Michael except boring cards—or with his dick. He was so odd; he liked Snap.

Her phone bleeped.

Trevor: *Don't do it again. I had to tell Cassie you hadn't got hold of me.*

What a bloody dickhead. Now Cassie would be arsey with her for not following the rules. Trevor would have done that on purpose, he liked getting her in the shit. She'd told him back when they were younger, before he'd got with Lisa, that she didn't want to go out with him when he'd asked her out. He'd never forgiven her. Once she'd found out he was her handler, things had been awkward for months.

Brenda: *Great. Cheers for that, knob rot.*

Trevor: *What did you fucking expect?*

Brenda: *Oh, bog off.*

Trevor and Lisa stared at each other, shrugged, then walked down the path. Lisa had read the messages along with Trevor, so wasn't it bothering her that Brenda had called her husband a rude name? The woman didn't know Trevor had fancied the pants off Brenda once upon a time, but still, surely she'd be curious.

The couple got into Trevor's Fiat and drove off. Crikey, Brenda had to get this mess sorted, couldn't put it off any longer, not if those two had been sent to find her. If there was an alert out on her, why hadn't Cassie texted, seeing as Lenny was feeling off colour?

She prodded at her screen and wrote to Cassie, giving her the address and adding: *Help needed, man down.*

She made herself a cuppa while she waited, filching the salt and pepper pots she'd long admired, fancy glass buggers that found a home inside her large handbag, destined for her dining room table. They looked like expensive crystal, and she'd feel dead posh using them. An old Walkman joined them, for nostalgia reasons, the bright-orange foam on the headphones bringing a flashback of her past, a time where she'd wanted a personal tape player so badly, but her parents hadn't had the money, not even for her birthday or Christmas. Food was more important, and that was scarce. She'd listened to Karen's from time to time, jealous as anything, and vowed that one day she'd own one.

And now she did.

By the time she'd got to the dregs of her tea, someone knocked again, and her phone went off at the same time.

Any more scares, and Brenda's heart wouldn't take it.

She read the message.

Cassie: *It's me.*

Inhaling deeply, letting it out through pursed lips to steady her poor nerves, Brenda opened the door. Cassie, her red hair bright in the light of the outside lamp, stepped inside, followed by that Jason Brenda didn't like or trust. She led them to the living room, her stomach churning. While she was in the autumn of her life and Cassie much younger, Brenda still feared her. Cassie had been pressed into her father's mould and took no prisoners. She had a nasty mouth on her these days, too, and didn't mind using it to bark at you.

Brenda would ordinarily bark back, but not to her.

"Fuck me," Cassie said, hands on hips, studying Michael. "This is a bit of a pisser, isn't it." She massaged her forehead, her long straight hair flopping over the back of her hand. "What happened?"

"We were shagging, and he died on me." Brenda shrugged. May as well tell it how it was. Cassie didn't like anyone beating around the bush, and the same went for Lenny, so Brenda shilly-shallying wasn't an option. "I've been sitting here for hours wondering what to do. Your dad being ill, I didn't want to bother him, and this isn't the usual scenario, is it. I mean, I wait a few weeks so it doesn't look off, they take the money out of the bank, I finally fuck them, then they die by themselves a couple of months later. They don't die when I'm *here*. This is a first for me, and I don't much want to repeat it."

She sounded callous, but Cassie would understand. A job was a job, a mark a mark. You did what you had to and moved on. Allowing yourself to feel tender emotions could be your downfall, and Brenda had no intention of going down (unless it was going down on an old man).

"Not sure what's the best bet here." Cassie bit her bottom lip.

Brenda hadn't expected her to admit that. Doing so was an old Cassie trait, not the new one she'd become. Over the past six months, Brenda had watched the young woman change, growing harder by the day, and she had a proper strong feeling that was Lenny's influence.

Cassie pinched her chin. "So...you dressed him again, I take it."

"Well, he only had his todger out, didn't he, so I didn't exactly dress—"

"All right." Cassie held up a hand and closed her eyes for a moment, then opened them and glared at Brenda. "Condom?" She gazed at Michael, her mouth downturned.

"No."

Cassie sighed. "So your DNA's on him. Clever."

Her sarcasm didn't hurt.

Brenda smiled, pleased she had a satisfactory comeback and wouldn't be in Cassie's bad books. "I washed him. What do you take me for, a novice?"

Jason shook his head. "It could still be on him. You're better off getting rid of him, Cassie."

Cassie clamped her jaw, a tic beating fast beside her eye. "I'll decide what I'm better off doing, thank you, and for now, it's ringing my mam." She walked out, her movements stiff.

Jason gawped after her, hatred on his reddened face. A public slap-down from Cassie would have upset him.

"You'd do well not to piss her off," Brenda told him. "She might be a woman, but she's Lenny through and through, just with tits. You keep sticking your oar in, she's going to bite your fucking head off, *and* you'll probably find yourself out on your ear. You might be her right hand now, but things can change."

Jason levelled a hard stare at her. "Sod off with your advice, Brenda. I'm not some wet-behind-the-ears pleb."

"Oh, but you are," she said. "It stands out a mile. The way to get around it, if you want her or Lenny to do what you suggest, is to make it seem like they thought of it. Follow that rule, and you won't go far wrong."

She had the urge to poke him in the eye but refrained. He was a jumped-up little dick who'd always grated on her nerves. His mother, Gina, thought she was better than everyone else, and it seemed to have rubbed off on him. She doubted he'd want people to know he'd been born with a plastic spoon in his mouth rather than silver, but he behaved as if he came from rich stock. That was Gina's doing. Since her old man had run off, she'd had airs and graces, doing herself up like some forties starlet, swanning up Brenda's street like the Queen.

"Whatever." He flashed his hand out to wave her off, shut her up.

Yes, a little dick.

"You'll learn." She flopped onto the armchair and lit another fag, smoking indulgently, acting as if he didn't stand there staring at a dead old man.

"I killed someone tonight," he said. "Same as you. Only, I blew his brains out. What did you do, shag him to death? Hardly anything to brag about, is it."

She laughed, long and hard. "Who's bragging? And, aww, is this your attempt at one-upmanship? You poor boy, feeling like you have to prove yourself." She threw him a savage look, sick of him, wishing he'd sod off out of it and leave this to the women. "What you need to prove is that you can play the long game, pal. And I *know* that's what you're doing. I've been in this business a fair while, and your goal is obvious. To fix anyone copping on, stay in the background. Observe. You'll get to the top quicker that way."

He eyed her funny, like she was shit on his shoe. "Why are you telling me this? Aren't you loyal to the Graftons?"

"Yep." She prepared her lie. "But I'm also loyal to whoever's likely to be paying my wages, and it seems that might be you a year or two down the line. *If* you can get Cassie to believe you want to go further with her. *If* you can make her think you love her. Isn't that what you're playing at?"

Jason turned to the doorway, cheeks flushing, hands clenching into fists.

Brenda chortled. "Thought so."

"Shut up. She's coming."

Brenda smiled to herself. She'd had him pegged from the start, knew he was a wrong 'un. She'd get him to trust her, admit what he was about, then she'd tell Lenny and Cassie, warn them they had a fox in the henhouse. "I won't say a word, but if you act on my advice and it works, you remember who gave it to you."

Cassie entered, her face pale, her eyes glistening. "We need to leave. Now."

"Shouldn't I hang around until someone collects the old fella, if that's what's occurring?" Brenda flicked ash into the saucer.

"No. You won't be needed." Cassie appeared distracted, her mind possibly full of this fuck-up and how to sweep it all under the carpet. "Where's the money?"

Brenda pointed to the mantel. "Up there. All twenty-two grand of it."

"Go and hide it under his mattress. I'll make sure you get paid anyroad. He's got a daughter, it's too risky. He dies on the day the money's withdrawn? Coppers will be all over the fucking place. We don't need it. *I* don't need it."

Brenda picked up on that, ever the vigilant soul. "Only you?"

Cassie nodded. "Yeah, only me."

"Lenny can deal—"

"Lenny nowt," Cassie spat out. "Dad's dead, Mam's just told me, so he won't be dealing with owt. It's me from now on, so do as you're told or face the consequences."

Chapter Six

At the rear of the meat factory, hidden from the main road out the front, Felix stared down at the body, the tarpaulin peeled back and flapping in the wind. It crackled from a particularly robust blast, and his hair swept up then flopped down into his eyes. "Fuck me. Poor Doreen when she hears about this."

He'd known her for years, what with living in the next street on the Barrington, and she always got her meat from their stall of a Saturday—pork chops, sausages, bacon, and a chicken or beef joint for the Sunday roast. She bought that lot then nipped over to the fruit and veg stall, picking up her carrots and whatnot.

She did amazing things with a fat carrot in the sack, liked an older man, so she'd said.

He blushed at the memory of letting her use veg on him while beneath her sweet-smelling sheets. The image of him, a cucumber, and Doreen telling him to 'hurry up and put it in' flashed through his mind.

Those were the days.

How he'd face her once they'd minced her son was anyone's guess. Normally, he didn't bat an eye, but…it was to do with Doreen. He'd shagged her for about six months around twenty years ago, a regular Saturday night treat, and Sunday mornings he'd taken Richie to the park to get him out from under her feet, so it felt a bit personal, this. The trouble was, only him and Ted did the body grinding as far as he knew, so he had no choice in the matter. The general workforce had no idea what went on in the dark hours.

"Fucking kid was destined for this." Ted gave the body a swift kick. "Never did like the nasty little runt. Do you remember when he nicked that fucking leg of lamb off us that time? Chancer. A weed, he reminded me of. Always there. Even when you pulled him up and tossed him away, the wanker came back."

"Hmm. Like all the kids, he could have made something of himself if he hadn't got roped into the life. It was the drugs that changed him. He got hooked and couldn't think straight. Never thought I'd hear of him stealing off his mother, but there you go. People change, and not for the better sometimes."

Felix and Ted had been no different, moving from Yorkshire to work in the meat factory, lured into the stickier side of the business by Lenny's spiel in The Donny: the money, the safety of being looked after by the gangster, and they should have known better, the age they'd been when he'd approached them. But he'd offered security, brighter skies. If you were lucky enough to get under his umbrella, no rain touched you.

Ted kicked Richie again—he had a bit of a mean streak every now and then. Felix didn't like him doing that. All he kept thinking about was the innocent kid Richie had been, not the fuck-up he'd become.

Ted stepped back. "Yeah, well, he had no ambition beyond easy money, selling drugs, but what a prize twazzock for doing that on Lenny's patch—for someone else. He should have pissed off to Sheffield and done it there."

Felix agreed on that score. "No brains." Guilt bothered him for saying that. Richie had brains, he'd been a bright lad, but drugs had dampened his intellectual spark. What a waste.

Ted toed a patch of concrete. "He won't have brains in half an hour. Anyroad, it looks like most of it has left his head already. It's probably decorating the squat wall."

"If Jason did him there."

Ted grunted. "No telling with that jumped-up prick. He's another one who needs to watch himself. Lenny won't put up with him keep creeping round Cassie. Jason's meant to be her right hand, not a bloody boyfriend."

Felix sniffed. "Let the kid make his own mistakes, and hopefully we'll get to mince him an' all." He sighed. "Come on. Let's get Richie inside."

Ted had already unlocked the door and disabled the alarm, plus he'd collected the trolley used specifically for bodies which they kept stored in a small room no one else but them, Lenny, Francis, and Cassie had access to, the same one the old mincer was in. The trolley stood beside the door now, so they hoisted the scrote up and dumped him on it. Nowt but a lightweight, this one, and they got on with pushing him inside, securing the place, then going to the mincer no longer used for saleable goods.

The machine was a big old thing, the steel dull after years of use, circular scrub marks from scouring pads marring the metal. Felix started her up, the grinding of the rotating blades loud. Lenny had named her Marlene, and she belched out a rumble of welcome, ready to do her thing.

Felix cringed a bit at the idea of where Doreen's son would end up but went to work, praying they'd get their Chinese after all. The Jade stayed open until midnight, so if they got their arses into gear, they'd make it.

Joe Wilson's pigs always acted up once they smelt the human mince, and they'd be getting excited any minute. He'd known Lenny since they were kids and didn't mind bodies being disposed of on Handel Farm. After all, it saved him a load of money in pig feed, and besides, he owed Lenny. Still. What that fella had done for him years ago… Well, Joe would never be able to pay him off. Some debts you couldn't stop shelling out for, could you. Some good deeds needed to be acknowledged, always.

"Who is it this time?" Joe asked.

Felix pulled out a ledge from the back of their van and pressed a red button to lower it, mince packed into a tall, half-a-metre-square transparent plastic container on top. It looked like a kitchen bin but with a flat lid. "Richie Prince."

"Doesn't surprise me." Joe shook his head. "Why didn't he learn? Lenny said he'd had a fair few warnings and it was coming up to the end of his patience. Who did him in? Cassie?"

"No, Jason." Ted coughed out 'twat'.

"Lenny wants to watch that one," Joe said, "and I've told him as much, but he won't have it. Thinks the sun shines out of the lad's arse. I've heard Jason's been lording it about a bit too much lately. Someone in The Donny had a gripe about it."

"Griping isn't good behind Lenny's back," Felix said, offering a warning frown.

Joe had a feeling that was a dig at him, but Lenny wouldn't mind him discussing things with these two. What he told them, he'd say it to Lenny, too.

Felix continued. "I heard his ticker's been playing him up again. He's not even old, our Len. Fifty-odd is nowt these days as you know yourself, Joe, so it's the stress of the business wreaking havoc, got to be. He needs to slow down a bit. Probably why he's got Cassie helping out. We saw her earlier as it happens." His phone buzzed, and he took it out of his pocket to read the screen.

While Felix gave his mobile his attention, Ted and Joe lugged the box over to one of the three pig pens inside the domed steel barn he had out the back of his farmhouse. The pigs snorted and trotted over, waiting by the fenced-off areas.

"Greedy fuckers," Ted said.

"Um..." Felix walked over and waved his phone about. "We need to get a move on and feed them, then we've got another body to collect."

Ted frowned. "You what?"

Joe was surprised at that. What the hell was going on tonight? A second body meant trouble. Did Lenny know about it? Was Cassie being bit heavy-handed, too enthusiastic, her new role going to her head?

Felix scratched his scalp and slipped his phone away. "Yeah, a decision's been made by Cassie. Some old boy's dead, being removed from his house as we speak. We have to take the van and meet up with the removal team, collect the body."

"Some old boy?" Joe asked.

That was unusual these days. Anyone old enough to have pissed Lenny off years ago was already dead, so someone else must have bugged him. Or Cassie by the sound of it.

Felix shrugged. "I don't ask questions, not with Cassie. Lenny, yeah, he's all right, we've known him so long he doesn't mind us being nosy, but her? She'd fair bite my head off, tell me to mind my own. Used to be a nice little girl all the time, but Lenny's trained her to be a right hard bitch while she's working. Still love her, though, cos she's lovely when she isn't on the job."

Now who's griping behind Lenny's back?

Joe glanced around the barn, eyeing the two other pig pens. It was one large one with fences dividing it into three. "Instead of spreading Richie out amongst them all, we'll split him between two pens, then the codger can go in with the third lot."

"It's going to be a late one," Felix grumbled. "*And* I definitely won't get my Chinese."

Joe smiled. "I'll order for one to be delivered here while you're with Marlene." Many a time he'd hankered after his dinner, only to be interrupted by Lenny wanting his advice or a chat about either the meat factory or the Barrington business.

Felix nodded. "Cheers, pal. Curry. Two for the price of one at the minute. And spring rolls."

They fed the animals in the first two pens, and in the third, loads of pigs grunted and squealed in complaint.

"Shut your faces, yours is coming in a bit," Ted barked.

Five minutes later, some pigs satisfied, the rest with a right old cob on, Joe loaded the empty plastic box into the van. Ted and Felix drove away, towards the Barrington. Joe left the barn, locked it up, and crossed the yard to the farmhouse. The kitchen light was on, and Lou, his wife, stood at the window looking out. The poor cow must feel bad every time the pigs got fed the mince, a reminder of what had happened years ago. He wished he could stop the meat coming here, but he couldn't, not while Lenny lived. The debt wasn't clear until the gangster died.

Her shape was still the same as the day he'd met her, rail thin on account of pecking at her food, a non-hungry bird who only ate to survive. She didn't enjoy what she put in her mouth, and he knew why she didn't indulge much. Time had healed his heartbreak somewhat, and he managed to laugh and act as if tragedy hadn't struck, but Lou, she always felt guilty every time she giggled.

She'd never get over it.

He stood in the mudroom and pulled off his wellies, placing them neatly along the right-hand wall beside Lou's and a smaller pink pair that had belonged to their daughter, Jessica. DCI Robin Gorley had given them and the rainbow coat back after the investigation, and Lou had washed them. No feet and legs filled those wellies anymore, hadn't for twenty-three years, but while Jessica was dead and buried, it didn't mean Lou could get rid of all their little girl's things.

Jessica's ghost lived on in those wellies, the waterproof, transparent raincoat with the rainbows all over it hanging from a hook above, and her room, full to bursting with her toys. They never got dusty, Lou went in and polished every week, and each night she drew the pink curtains and popped the lamp on, and each morning she opened them and switched the lamp off. She pretended a lot, did Lou, couldn't get past their child being gone.

Joe entered the kitchen, trying not to notice the gleaming tears in Lou's eyes, but it was the same every time the meat came, and tonight she'd have a double whammy.

"They'll be back," he said. "Sorry." He picked his phone up from the table to ring the Jade.

She tucked strands of greying hair behind her ears, the ever-present shadows beneath her hollow eyes bringing pain to his soul. If he could turn back time and make everything okay, he would.

"Don't be sorry. I like the reminder," she whispered.

He stared, shocked. "That Jess is gone?"

"No, every time the pigs eat mince, I remember the feeling of justice being served back then."

Joe swallowed, alarmed by the venom in Lou's voice, wary of the narrowing of her eyes and the firm set of her mouth. She'd never mentioned how she'd felt before, not regarding the meat, and he'd always assumed it crushed her time and again. All these years, and he hadn't known she must have enjoyed it.

Was that something for him to worry about?

"I never want the debt paid," she said, gaze out there on the pig barn. "If Lenny goes before me, tell Cassie you'll keep taking the meat. I want to see it fed to those beasts over and over again."

Chapter Seven

Jason was pissed off driving towards Lenny's gaff. As soon as they'd left Michael Whatever's place, Cassie had made a phone call to the removal team without discussing it with him first. She'd taken over Lenny's role already, and the man hadn't been dead five minutes. The old fella Brenda had killed was being extracted from the property. Jason could only imagine Cassie's logic in doing that. If the bloke was missing, none of Brenda's DNA could be found on him. Brenda had been nicked in her time so had a record, albeit from years ago, so what about her fingerprints all over the bloke's fucking house, let alone her mess on his dick?

That question had been answered after Cassie had sent a message to someone. Probably Felix or Ted, warning them they'd need to fire Marlene up again tonight. Cassie and Lenny had let him know who Marlene really was a couple of months ago, and he had to admit, the bullshit Lenny had spread about her yonks ago had scared him while he'd been growing up. He'd believed the mincer was a bloody woman.

Cassie had phoned the cleaning crew next and told them to set the man's house alight once the body removal people had been and gone, taking the money envelope out from under his mattress first.

Typical female, changing her mind regarding that later down the line. Earlier, she'd worried about coppers sniffing round about the withdrawal, although it made sense to steal it now. Saved it going up in flames, didn't it.

"What do you mean, you're still at the squat?" Cassie had said to one of the crew. She'd given Jason a glare that would wither anyone else. "How much mess *is* there? Christ."

That didn't sound right. Jason had done a bit of cleaning at the squat. And what was she playing at with this fire business? The old boys' house was mid-terrace, for Pete's sake. What about the ones either side? They'd have other ancient grannies and whatever in them, probably in bed by now.

He'd had to butt in. "Arson in a terrace? Fuck me, Cass. *Think.*"

She'd listened and said into her phone, "Light it and knock the neighbours up, get them out. Wear face coverings."

Jason had hidden a smug smile.

Now, he thought of what Brenda had said and kept his mouth shut. She had a point. If he remained in the background, putting spanners in the works from there, Cassie wouldn't suspect him. In the forefront, he'd be her right hand, offering simple advice like he had about the fire, be someone she turned to, and eventually, she'd see sense and go out with him, have a relationship. She had to, else his plan to take over wouldn't succeed. He wasn't stupid enough to think he could steal the Barrington under his own steam. For one, Lenny's men would stay loyal to her, and two, he'd be signing his own death warrant. While he only owned a Bic to do that at the minute, he intended on having an ink pen with a fancy nib to sign Cassie's later on. A Mountblanc, gold-coated, retailing at nigh on seven hundred quid.

He'd be rich or die trying.

Unable to stick to his recent promise to keep his nose out, he asked, "Everything okay?" Stupid question. Of course it wasn't okay, her old man had just died. *Shit.* "I mean with work, not Lenny."

"It's fine. Keep your hooter out."

He had no choice but to let that slide, given the circumstances. "I gathered you're sorting the old man. Michael."

She stared ahead, jaw clamped.

Bollocks. He'd pushed it again, sent her inside that stupid shell of hers. Why couldn't he step back and do what Brenda had advised? Why did he always have to *know* everything?

Because I need to know so I can plan.

"Sorry," he said. "I'm worried about you." *Yeah, that's it, play that card, make her think you give a shit.* "You've got a lot on your plate, what with your dad and—"

"He taught me to file emotions away when it comes to work. Said they cloud the issue. I'll grieve him in my own time, but while there's shit to be sorted, I'll sort it. He'd want me to do that. If he's up there watching me now, you can bet he's egging me on, telling me I'm doing the right thing."

You tell yourself that, love. When you're dead, that's the end. No Heaven. Lenny won't be watching over you any more than I'm Prince Harry.

She paused to sigh, and he reckoned it was in irritation, being bugged by him, her having to explain herself when she undoubtedly didn't want to, yet at the same time had to, establishing the pecking order. Like he was some gimp who didn't know what it was.

"I won't deviate from what he taught me," she went on. "So while you might not agree about Michael, I don't give a toss—I *can't* give a toss. I learnt from the best, and with Brenda's freedom on the line, I took the correct route. She's a high source of income—protect the revenue, *always*. Everything to do with her will be minced or burnt."

"It's just the police involvement with a fire…"

She sighed yet again. "*Fuck off* and mind your own beeswax. If you want to be my right hand, play by *my* rules, the Grafton rules, not your own, or you'll find yourself inside Marlene before you can blink." She stared across at him. "And that isn't a threat."

Gordon Bennett, Cassie was a right hard bitch these days, and he'd underestimated her. Many a minute he'd contemplated her reaction to her father's death, how she'd crumble and turn to him, her face buried against his chest, fingers gripping the back of his suit jacket, and telling him she was unable to run the business because grief wore her down. How wrong he'd been. Like people said, she *was* Lenny through and through, and he'd do well to remember that.

She was going to make things difficult, bodge up his plans.

With a right grump on, he drove down her street, envious. Although it was on the Barrington, it was one of the new builds out the back. Sculptor's Field remained, but the ones farther back were no more, Joe selling them to Lenny, who'd then sold them for profit to a developer, the cheeky fucker. They were now filled with fifty new roads. That manky horse thing was still there, a shrine to Jessica Wilson. A couple of metres surrounding it had white posts with chains linking them around it, and on the plinth a gold plaque had been placed, In Loving Memory, that sort of shite. Lenny had bought Sculptor's Field, too, finding the previously unknown owner and offering him a wedge.

So many people caved when presented with money.

Jason had gone to playgroup with Jessica, although he couldn't remember her. Many people around here spoke of her like she was some kind of angel, the women misty-eyed, the men all keyed-up as if the bloke who'd killed her was still out there, ready for them to find, and if they did, they'd rip him to shreds and string his entrails up on The Beast.

Pricks, the lot of them. His mam had always detested living on the Barrington with all the morons, but she loved their house, said she'd hate to leave it, but the fire in his belly to take over was in part so he could move her from her two-bed council place and into one of the swanky efforts he drove past now.

It was a different world here.

He turned into Lenny's drive—Francis's now, he supposed—gravel crackling beneath his tyres, and stopped outside the Georgian-like structure. A car belonging to Dr Flemming had been parked haphazardly, as if he'd arrived and wanted to rush indoors, unheeding of whether his vehicle was an obstruction. Flemming was a nice bloke, one of the partners at the local surgery. Jason had shown him his dick once, the diagnosis those sexual warts, and he'd had a mad go at the bird who'd given them to him. He hoped Flemming didn't spout any inuendoes once they got inside.

Of course he bloody won't. What's the matter with you?

Jason shook that out of his head and stared at the house. All the lights blazed in a 'fuck global warming' kind of way, and rudeness towards the environment got on his nerves. When he lived here, he'd soon sort such a waste of energy out.

Cassie left the car, and he went to follow suit, unclipping his seat belt.

She poked her head back in the passenger side. "Thanks. That'll be all for tonight, unless I need you for owt."

She closed the door and walked off.

Such a cheeky bitch.

Jason stifled the urge to go after her, insist she needed him *now*, not later, then remembered he had to go and have a sniff around Richie Prince's bedsit. There was white powder for the taking, and it'd be right at home up Jason's nose. He could do with a treat after the evening he'd had.

Fuck me, what a night.

He reversed onto the street and took his time about driving along, admiring the houses, all set back from the pavement, all sequestered behind high hedges pruned to perfection, a gardener or two paid to do it, no doubt. Christ, he couldn't wait to get his mother into one of them, and he knew exactly how he was going to do it, too. She deserved the best. He'd hire a cleaner, a chef even, so she didn't have to lift a finger. She'd never belonged on the crustier side of the Barrington, had always come across as a cut above the benefit scroungers, even when she'd been skint as arseholes with Dad and he'd nicked things for their house, furniture and stuff. Jason wanted her to live out her remaining days, of which he hoped there'd be many, in luxury.

He cruised into Old Barrington as it was now known, past the high-rises that Lenny had somehow bought. Jason would love to know how the younger Lenny had built his business up from small-time bollocks to a massive empire. He had to be a millionaire a couple of times over, and the cash called to Jason in a way nowt else had.

He wanted it. Every last penny.

Down Bladen Avenue he turned, the mankiest street on the estate, where people lived hand to mouth, using the rent money from Housing Benefit to supplement their dole-laden spending habits—weed, coke, fags, booze, a small shopping delivery from the Iceland van—then finding themselves on the arse end of an eviction order once the landlords didn't receive their due. It was stupid, Jason reckoned, that the rent got paid direct to claimants these days, trust put in them to pass it on and not dip their thieving fingers into it.

Fucking losers.

He stopped the car down the side of the bedsit block Richie had lived in. Darkness hid his vehicle, the bulb from the lamppost there probably smashed by bored kids who'd most likely laughed their heads off when they'd broken it. He thanked them for their mischief and got out of the car, moving to the corner of the building. A quick look around showed him no one was out and about, not Doreen, not Mam, not even Lenny's drug runner by the wonky street sign, huddled up inside his puffa parker.

He fished Richie's keys out of his pocket and inserted one into the main foyer door, again no light on in there, the residents either too skint or plain not bothered about replacing the bulb. He stepped inside, and his previous assumption was proved wrong as brightness filled the space. Must be a motion sensor.

Jason took to the stairs and, on the landing, stared at the one open door at the end—the shared bathroom—then the three closed ones. Richie's was in the middle, so he tried a couple of keys in the Yale, getting the right one on the fourth attempt. Inside, he closed himself in, retching at the stale stench, and went straight for the living side of the room in search of the legendary safe from Argos.

Christ, what a shithole. Richie hadn't been a fan of keeping things nice and tidy then. It was a wonder he'd found owt in this dump. Jason had to move discarded clothes, pinching them with finger and thumb they were that rotten, some with hardened areas, and he dreaded to think what *that* was from. They clearly hadn't been washed in ages.

He turned his attention to the bedroom area. A single divan with drawers underneath drew him, and he threw aside full carrier bags of God knew what, boots, a pair of trainers, and the battery charger for Richie's silly motorised bike.

Drawers open, he spied the safe and hefted it out. It wasn't that heavy, so he placed the bike battery on top and carried them from the bedsit, the door snicking closed behind him. Out into the darkness he went, around the corner and into his car, the stolen goods on the passenger seat. He smiled—maybe he'd get more than fifty quid for the bike now he had the charger—and chose the most obvious key on the ring to check if it fitted the safe. Saved him fucking about trying all sorts of code combinations on the door's keypad, didn't it.

The key worked and, in the glow of the interior car light, he opened the door.

He'd hit paydirt. The safe not only contained weed, coke, and pills, but cash, a nice bundle of it Richie hadn't passed on to whoever had employed him to sell gear.

"I'll be having that, thanks." Jason smiled again, so hard it hurt his cheeks. He'd pay Mam's rent for the next couple of months and buy her a new dress.

Life was getting better.

Chapter Eight

Cassie sat on the leather sofa in their big living room now Dad's body had been taken away. Dr Flemming had arranged it all, and she'd watched alongside Mam, the front door opening then Dad being carried out on a stretcher beneath an NHS waffle-weave blanket. It was surreal, as if it wasn't really happening, but it had, it still was, an hour after his departure.

He was gone, and now she was the queen of the Barrington. She didn't want the title, needing her father back to continue his reign instead. He wasn't supposed to be dead yet, it was too soon, and how was she supposed to keep her monster in play when she wanted to scream and cry and grieve for the man she'd looked up to?

Mam had been crying steadily, silently though, tears falling without sobs or hitching shoulders. She was a strong woman and, like Cassie, would properly mourn behind a closed bedroom door. Cassie didn't look forward to wrenching cries filtering along the landing, and she'd cry quietly herself, not wanting to put more pressure on Mam. She shouldn't have to worry about Cassie being upset, not on top of her own devastation.

They'd expected this outcome, of course they had, Dad's previous heart attack something they'd kept quiet about, and had prayed an operation would come sooner rather than later. As far as most were aware, he'd been under the weather and Cassie was standing in for him. Of course, those who worked for him knew he had a dodgy heart, but they weren't about to tell all and sundry. Tonight, he hadn't had any chest pains before she'd left to meet Jason, just that funny turn where he'd gone giddy and had to sit down or fall down, saying it was only indigestion and blaming the pastry he'd had for lunch, sausage rolls.

The first small attack had been a warning for him to stop stressing, his body's way of telling him to slow down completely, but he'd ignored the advice and still kept his hand in every now and then, and now look, he'd suffered a massive one, Mam all alone to deal with it, halfway through their Chinese, until Cassie had arrived.

The cartons and a bag of unopened prawn crackers still littered the worktop. Dad's fork had fallen to the floor. She could only imagine the scene.

He'd have hated himself for putting that on his wife, her seeing him go out like that. Even her being there to witness it was something he'd said he didn't want. Cassie hadn't asked how it had gone down, not the full story. She didn't want the visuals, the knowledge that he'd definitely been in pain, which he would have been, or perhaps it had been too quick. On the phone, while Cassie had been with Brenda and Jason, Mam had just said his heart had given out and he was gone.

"You've got everything under control?" Mam rose from the armchair and moved to the window. She parted the grey crushed-velvet curtains to look out. "He'd want you focused, ready to go by yourself."

Cassie nodded. "I was working when you rang me, even on the way over once you'd told me, mopping up some of Brenda's mess, and as for the shit Jason pulled earlier…"

Mam turned, the poised and elegant Francis Grafton, and faced Cassie, her face wet with tears. She wiped them using a scrunched-up tissue, and Cassie reckoned now the tears were on it, that tissue was the only sign, apart from her red-rimmed eyes, that Mam had lost the love of her life. Was she as scrunched-up inside? Was she longing to scream and rail, to curse God or whatever higher power for taking her husband away too early? Was she cursing Him for going against what Dad would want by allowing her to see it all play out?

"I'm going to do this with you," Mam said. "Push grief aside and advise you until you're fully ready to go out there on your own. More crying can wait. We have to keep the business running as if he were here. This is why he made you his right hand early, retiring Glen Maddock, so you'd know everything, know what to do."

"It'll get us through, that will, doing what he'd want." And if Cassie needed more advice, she could always visit Glen.

Mam nodded. "We'll be doing it for your father. His wishes granted."

As if Dad himself had said that, calming Cassie, the lump in her throat diminished, the stinging in her eyes stopped. She had to force herself to remain strong, like Mam was doing for her. Together, for now, they'd run the Barrington,

Cassie as the front woman, Mam instructing in the background, and woe betide anyone who thought they were weak because of their gender. Like Cassie had vowed before, she'd be better than the indomitable Lenny, she'd get people fearing her more than him. She might not have the power of a man's punch, but she'd been trained in martial arts and could kick anyone's arse.

She was her father's daughter, and there was no way she'd let him down.

"Kitchen," Mam said, no-nonsense. She dropped the tissue in the wicker bin. "We need coffee. The death certificate and other bullshit can wait until tomorrow. I want to know what's what from your side of tonight. My side? He's dead, end of."

That wasn't really how Mam felt, she was just showing Cassie how to behave. There was no way on this earth 'end of' was the truth. It would *never* end, Mam's pining for him, her missing him. It'd last until her dying day.

Cassie followed her and sat at the island. She remembered the times she'd made cakes there as an older kid after they'd moved in, allowed to hold the eggs until Mam had finished smoothing the butter and sugar. She vaguely recalled doing it at their former house, too, the one on Old Barrington. What a great childhood she'd had on this estate, loved so much by Lenny and Francis, never bullied because no one would dare. But they'd whispered about her father, saying he was tough and scary, and she hadn't known what they'd meant until Dad had explained the business once she was old enough to take it. She'd grown up now, and while the weight of grief and

152

full responsibility weighed heavy, she'd straighten her shoulders, get her business head on, and push forward.

Her true soft centre must be hidden from everyone. She'd fly with wings of steel.

Mam made the coffee and brought it over. She busied herself cleaning up the Chinese remnants, picking up the fucking dropped fork, and Cassie told her the basics about tonight.

Mam sighed, sitting opposite. She took a sip of coffee. Swallowed. Rubbed an eye that looked sore from crying. "So what about Doreen? Have you actioned owt there? She needs to be told Richie's dead."

Cassie had forgotten to do that, and she cursed herself. But she wouldn't tell her mother. She'd lie instead. Dad had lied sometimes, she was sure of it, to protect her and Mam, and himself—he didn't like admitting he'd fucked up. Cassie didn't either. "I wanted to discuss it with Dad, but..."

"Right, let's think as if we're in his head. Would he send an anonymous note or go to her himself in this situation? Richie was selling on his patch without his permission, so it's a given he'd be told off. Doreen doesn't like drugs, she kicked Richie out because of peddling, so it won't come as a surprise to her to find her son was dealt with. How many warnings did Jason give Richie?"

"Several, although he was only supposed to take him to the squat and frighten the shit out of him this evening, up the scare factor. I'm going to bring in a new rule. One verbal warning, and the second involves Marlene."

"I agree. Too many warnings invites them to take the piss. Your dad was soft on that score. So why did Jason shoot Richie?"

Cassie ground her teeth for a moment. "Because Richie called him a prick."

"Excuse me?" Mam closed her eyes for a second as if wanting to explode. "Who have you chosen for your right hand going forward now your father has no say?"

"Jason."

Mam's eyebrows lifted. "Is that wise?"

"He's been with me for months. While he gets on my wick, always poking his nose in, we work okay together. I wouldn't want to train anyone else—Dad put him with me anyroad, so he must have thought he was okay."

"Right, well, for what it's worth, let it be on record that I think, with his impulses, shown tonight by killing Richie for something ridiculous like name-calling, Jason's one for you

155

to watch. I didn't always agree with your dad, you know."

"Noted." Cassie sighed. "So back to Doreen. Sounds to me like you think she needs a personal visit."

"I do. She won't say a word about it to anyone else. Lou once told me Doreen is excellent at keeping secrets."

"Maybe if Dad were alive, she'd be too scared to blab, but with me in charge…"

"Then threaten her. Make her see you mean it. Show her your gun, act emotionless, whatever, just keep her gob shut." Mam sounded sharp, as if grief had razored her edges.

"Fine. I'll go after we've finished this chat."

"Next up." Mam sipped, the cup shaking a bit.

Poor cow, trying to hold it together. "Ted and Felix have taken care of Richie, and they'll do the same for Michael, Brenda's body."

"Not the woman's fault the old man had a heart attack—which is only what we can assume. If he was well enough to go to town and withdraw all that money, she wouldn't have known to make herself scarcer yet. She likes to be out of the way once they're on their last legs." Mam's eyebrows drew together. "I have no idea how she shags them all, though. I mean…"

Cassie swallowed a harsh retort—she'd never understand how Mam didn't mind living off the proceeds yet complained about the prostitution side of things, a faint tinge of disgust for those who sold themselves. Mam was great but had double standards, and while Cassie would normally bite her head off and remind her that some people didn't have the luxury of a steady job, tonight wasn't that night. Cassie felt for the sex workers, how they'd had to choose that particular path, and she'd do her best to sway Mam's thinking on that as time went by.

"It's what she's agreed to do, Mam, and she gets paid well for it. I've got one of the cleaners coming here later to deliver Michael's envelope with the cash in it. I'll get it laundered then pass her the usual. She did the graft so earned it."

Mam's brief nod ended that part of the conversation. "What else needs discussing?"

"The fire. The cleaners, when they finally leave the squat, which is probably about now, will go to Michael's, get the envelope out, and torch the place. Don't worry, the neighbours will be alerted—you have Jason to thank for that one because I wasn't thinking straight at the time I gave the order to burn it down."

"Understandable, but you need to work on your emotions."

Cassie hid another snap. "Dad had only just died."

"I realise that, but like I said, work on them." Mam shrugged. "It's not like you won't get enough practise at the moment. If you can run the Barrington while grieving, you can do anything."

They stared at each other across the island, mutual grief floating, silent, unseen, but right there in their hearts and the tears filling their eyes.

Cassie couldn't hold the look for long and moved back to business. "I took some drug money from Li Jun at the Jade and dropped it off with the supplier — this was before we went to see Brenda."

"Right."

"The supplier understands he's now been paid in advance for half of the next batch. Li Jun had a good week, shifting all that gear I left him with—stuff that would normally last a month. Seems more people than we realised like a bit of sniff with their chow mein." Cassie stared at her untouched coffee. "I think that's everything. Once Felix or Tom let me know they've dropped Michael off and the pigs have had a feed, and I've got back from Doreen's, I can get some sleep once I've filled in the ledger." She recalled having to give out a telling off in The Donny. "Oh, Trevor and Lisa Bayliss."

"What about them?"

"Gossiping about work in The Donny. I had a go at them."

Mam's lips pursed, her eyes flashing. "Of all the *stupid* bloody things. What were they saying?"

"No names were mentioned, but they talked about Brenda not checking in. She hadn't let anyone know she was okay."

Mam bobbed her head. "Makes sense, with Trevor being her handler to save your dad having to keep track of everyone and everything. If they do it again, go for them. An official verbal warning, then they meet Marlene, like you said."

"I have to admit, if it wasn't for them gassing, I might not have known about the old man dying until it was too late—like Trevor finding out first. Lisa seemed like she was telling me it was Trevor's fault for chatting about it in public, but she never told him to shut up before I butted in, so she's as guilty as him in my book."

Mam gave one of her rigid glares. "Take no prisoners, Cass, you march them straight to the guillotine. People need to know you mean what you say, that you're not a pushover. They'll try it with your dad gone, but I'm telling you now, be tougher, make an example of those who test the boundaries. Marlene will see a lot of people before folks get the message, but that's neither here nor there. You're a Grafton, and they need to respect that. No holding back, my girl. You're the boss."

Chapter Nine

The Barrington Life – Your Weekly

JESSICA WILSON FOUND DEAD!

Karen Scholes – All Things Crime in our Time
Sharon Barnett – Chief Editor

SPECIAL LATE-EVENING EDITION – SUNDAY JUNE 29th 1997

You may already be aware, as news spreads fast on the Barrington, but we're sorry to announce that little Jess Wilson was found by me, Karen Scholes, late Sunday aft. Some bastard had left her by The Beast on Sculptor's Field, dumped her there, and I can't tell you how distraught I am about that. That tiny tot had done nowt to deserve what happened, she was a beautiful part of the patch's family, and we will never forget her. Like I said before, if you know who did this, get in touch. If you're harbouring the bastards, shame on you, and I hope you rot in Hell.

Lenny will be looking into buying not only The Beast but the land it sits on, and anyone who'd like to pay their respects over the coming years can do so there. Don't go at the minute, though, the place is crawling with pigs as I type this, and I don't mean the ones belonging to Joe that have snouts. They're on their knees, searching for clues.

Well, it's a bit fucking late for that, isn't it?

I had to stay and give my account of how I found her, and tomorrow I go to the cop shop for the official statement. I don't know how she died, there was no blood and she looked asleep, but she had all the clothes on she was taken in, her hair still in that ponytail. Maybe she was cared for, who knows.

Please, if anyone knows owt, get in contact. We need to find the wankers, so keep your eyes and ears open. Whoever it is, if you're reading this, time's ticking, pal. We will come for you, we will catch you, and as God is my witness, you will pay for what you've done. You've robbed parents of their child, and for what? Some sick game you're playing?

In light of that, Barrington people, please, please keep a proper eye on your kiddies. We don't want a repeat of what's happened. Children are precious, they shouldn't be snatched from their father with a shotgun pointed at them. They shouldn't be left by that fucking Beast as if they're nowt but rubbish.

Anyone who'd like to contribute to the Jessica Wilson funeral fund can come to me or Sharon and drop your donations off. Lenny will foot the basic bill, but we want this princess to have a good send-off, so we're asking for cash to hire a horse and carriage hearse. Dig deep, as much as you can spare. One of our own has gone, and it breaks my heart. Let's send her to the angels in style.

Marcus James bit his scabby fingernails one after the other, spitting each one out onto the carpet. His thumb bled where he'd chomped too far down, but that was the least of his worries. The late-evening edition of The Barrington Life *had arrived, and that version only dropped through the letterbox when serious shit was going down. The sight of it had frightened him witless, his knees going from under him.*

The thing was, he knew who'd taken Jess. Marcus had been the one in the back of the fucking van, and now he reckoned, with there being a body, it was only a matter of time before the coppers or Lenny came knocking at his mam's weather-beaten door.

A body. This was more than serious shit. This was him going to prison for longer than his part in the kidnap. This was lags beating him up on the daily, reminding him with every rise of the sun that he was a scummy kid snatcher.

This was torture.

Shite. How had it happened? Jess was supposed to be held for ransom, not dumped near that weird Beast—dead, of all things. The plan was that Jess would be taken first, then if Lenny paid the ransom, which he would have once he'd received the note asking for it, she'd be returned, dropped off at Handel Farm in the middle of the night, the pigs grunting to let her parents know she was home. Alive. A month later, Cassie Grafton would be the next snatch and a bigger payout. Now, there was no money and no kid, nowt to barter for, because Lenny and Francis wouldn't be letting Cassie out of their sight.

He'd been told not to use Mam's house phone to contact the brains behind the scam, so he picked up the mobile he'd been given and prodded the buttons to get the thing to work. Only one number in his contact list, so he pressed to connect the call.

Brains answered on the second ring. "What."

"What do you mean, what? The kid's been found on Sculptor's Field, you fucking moron."

"Yeah, just read The Life. *I wondered where she'd got to."*

Marcus's skin went cold. "You what?"

"The little cow woke up, didn't she, and got out while I was on the crapper. I'd forgotten to lock my office door after I'd checked on her. That stuff I bought

to knock her out wasn't strong enough. Phenergan or whatever the hell it's called. Charlene swore it would work."

"You told Charlene—our mate Charlene?"

"Of course I didn't, I asked her as if your cousin wanted to know for calming down her nippers. I'm not stupid."

"Well, you could have fooled me, seeing as the kid got out. How did she even open the front door?"

"I must have left it open when Karen Scholes knocked asking her stupid questions. You know, when she handed over the first news article earlier in the day."

Marcus had already phoned Brains about that. He'd shit himself when Karen had rung the bell while Mam dished up the roast around one. Karen had asked him about Jess, whether he'd seen the kid, and Marcus had said no, he hadn't, what would he want with a littlun?

He'd taken the flyer off her and gone back inside, reading it on the way to the kitchen. His guts had gone at the mention of Lenny Grafton. That was Marcus's one misgiving, them planning to ask Lenny to cough up the ransom. You didn't cross that bloke, and they must be mad to even consider it.

Yet here they were, the kid wandering off and ending up dead.

"How come she died?" he asked. "Like, the medicine couldn't have harmed her because she trotted off in them wellies. What else did you do to her?"

"Nowt! Maybe she fell off that horse thing in the field."

That was a load of old guff. "How would she have even been able to climb on the plinth? She's only three, and it's too high."

"I don't fucking know, do I."

Marcus wasn't sure whether to believe him. Kids didn't just snuff it, did they. "So what do we do now?"

"Abort the mission. Stay under the radar. Then we'll move on like we would have done before, snatch Grafton's brat in a few months when his guard's down."

Marcus didn't want any part of this, not now the child had carked it. The police would give more of a toss with a body on their hands, and Lenny would be gunning for them. Marcus didn't reckon he could handle the stress of it. He'd already bitten all his nails off, for God's sake. What was next, his toes?

"Find someone else," he said. "I can't do this."

"You'll miss out on a big payday. Grafton will hand over loads. Like, fifty thousand at least."

"It's not worth it."

"You're mental to turn it down."

Marcus couldn't be swayed. "Maybe, but good luck if you carry on. Did you respray the van?"

"Yeah, this morning."

That was something then. The bloke on the other end of the line, known as The Mechanic, owned a garage, had access to all manner of shit to do with vehicles, and no one would question him having a van on the site. He'd nicked it—the original had been red—then resprayed it white so it blended in with all the others of that colour on the streets. The second spray was going to be black, but whether he'd stuck with that Marcus didn't know, nor did he care anymore.

"Right." Marcus sucked on the blood from his thumb. "Well, like I said, good luck."

The Mechanic coughed. "I don't need to warn you to keep your gob shut, do I."

"Nope."

"Good."

Marcus ended the call and thought about that. All right, The Mechanic was a right dodgy bastard, someone to be wary of, but Grafton was someone else altogether. Marcus weighed it up, The Mechanic versus Grafton, and he knew which side his bread was buttered.

He checked the bottom of The Life *where all the phone numbers were—Karen's, Sharon's, Lenny's, and the direct line to the police station dealing with this monumental fuck-up. He stuffed the piece of paper in his jeans pocket, slid his trainers on, grabbed the mobile, and left the house to Mam shouting, "Get me a pint of milk if you pass the shop, will you?"*

Outside, people gathered in the dark, discussing The Life *and the terrible news it had brought. He hated the sound of women crying and their gossiping tongues, dissecting what could have happened to Jess and what Lenny would do if he found who was responsible. Marcus had thought much the same while he'd chomped on his fingernails, but he hadn't gone downstairs to gabble about it with Mam, had he. No, it was obscene to talk about Jess that way.*

He was drawn to the edge of the Barrington and stood in an alley between houses, staring out over Sculptor's Field. Lights had been set up, big fuckers on metal poles, the grass and The Beast in full view along with some coppers in uniform and others in white outfits inside a bowed, flapping cordon. This was all too real, too nasty, and he turned away to walk back along the street he'd come down to find a safe place to use the mobile.

That safe place was beneath a tree a short distance from one of the three little shops dotted about on the estate. The branches and leaves drooped, heavy with rain from the recent downpour, one he'd listened to in his room, the fingertip taps of it on his window giving him the creeps.

He leant on the trunk and took the mobile out of his pocket, jabbed at the button by feel alone to switch it on. The small screen lit up, and he tugged the piece of paper from his pocket and checked the number he wanted. He pressed it into the handset and paused with his thumb hovering over the connect button. Once he did this, it was over. If The Mechanic squealed and dropped Marcus in it…

Marcus might as well dig his own grave now.

He touched the button. Held the phone to his ear. Three rings.

"Who is this?" Grafton barked.

Marcus jumped and prepared to change his voice, get it all gravelly so it wouldn't be recognised, not that he'd ever spoken to Lenny before, but whatever. Best to disguise it. "I've got news on the kid. Jess."

"What is it?"

"You need to pay The Mechanic a visit."

"You fucking what?" Lenny exploded.

"Yes, him, the one who valets your cars and shit. The shotgun's in a locked filing cabinet in his garage, same with the boilersuit and the balaclava. The van's

round the back—it'll not be white now, though, maybe black."

Lenny's heavy breathing sounded ominous. "What about the bloke in the back?"

"Got to go."

Marcus severed the connection and switched the mobile off, shaking all over. He opened the back, hands trembling, took the SIM out, and pushed it into the mud beneath the grass. Stamped it down. He thought of his own balaclava, at home in his drawer, and would need to get rid of it, drop it in a bin somewhere, maybe go to Sheffield on the bus and dispose of it there. He had no doubt that The Mechanic was going to get a visit tonight, and he didn't have to imagine what would happen to him.

Marcus just had to hope he didn't meet the same fate.

Chapter Ten

Doreen stared at Cassie on her doorstep and *knew* something was amiss. She idly wondered if her past had finally caught up with her and Cassie was here to ask a lot of intrusive questions, ones she'd rather not answer. Not only was it late—the doorbell had got her out of bed, and Harry had woken up, asking, "Where the bloody hell are you going, Dor?"—but to have a Grafton of any description around yours didn't bode well unless you were in with them.

Doreen wasn't. Harry wasn't. And if rumours were right, Richie wasn't. The silly lad had been stepping on Lenny's patch selling drugs for someone other than Lenny, and Doreen wanted no part of it. Her brother, God rest his wicked, drug-withered soul, had been an addict, and she'd watched him steal from Mam in their youth to fund the habit. All her jewellery had been swiped, gone into his filthy pocket then passed to a pawnshop bloke, the proceeds buying his gear. Heroin wasn't cheap, and while gossip had it that Richie only sold weed and coke—*only*, like it was nowt—it was still revolting, and she wouldn't have him beneath her roof if that was his game.

Besides, he was old enough and ugly enough to look out for himself, so he could stay in that scummy bedsit along the road and leave her alone. Of course, him living so close meant she still saw him from time to time, but it was like they weren't related, didn't know each other from Adam or that evil Eve. That was what happened when you put your foot down and your only child took umbrage.

Tough shit.

She'd learnt to harden her heart, especially once Richie had stolen from her. It was her brother all over again, and no good would come of him.

"What do you want?" Doreen folded her arms over her red fleece dressing gown fronts to keep the damn things from falling open and displaying her wrinkled, drooping wares. She slept in her birthday suit, had lost the belt for the gown, and suspected Sally from next door had nicked it off the washing line the week before last.

Sally had a dressing gown exactly like it, so there was the proof.

"I need to come in," Cassie said.

Doreen sagged against the doorframe, her knees going a tad weak. This had to be about Richie, and by God, she couldn't be doing with it. Doreen and Harry weren't bad people and hadn't given Lenny cause to send his daughter here, so yes, Richie was the culprit. "Oh fuck. What's he gone and done?"

Cassie's expression, unreadable, had Doreen wondering how the redhead could be so stone-faced. Like The Beast, she was, the same white, too. She was what, in her mid-twenties? How had she learnt the art of hiding her feelings so well lately? It must be Lenny's influence, because

Cassie had always been a sunny child and teenager. Mind you, that Francis was a hard bint and no mistake, likeable, though, so Cassie had good teachers, and it was no wonder she looked at Doreen the way she was.

"Like I said, I need to come in." Cassie gave a tight smile, as if it pained her to do so, and it didn't sit right on her face.

Doreen had smiled like that once or twice in her lifetime, mainly when belt-stealing Sally came round for a cup of sugar or some PG. Doreen never gave her those precious pyramid teabags. She kept a box of Tesco's own in her cupboard for the likes of the scrounging neighbours and a sugar stash that wasn't Tate & Lyle, thank you very much. The finer things in life she kept for herself.

She sighed and stepped back. "If he's caused trouble, my lad, it's nowt to do with me. Why you'd be here is a Scooby Doo mystery, because I kicked him out, told him not to come back. Whatever he does is no concern of mine, his choices belong to him, so if you're here to ask me to get him in line, the answer's no."

Cassie walked inside. She whiffed of some expensive perfume or other, a brand Doreen would never be able to afford on her part-time betting shop wage. Eau de Snooty Rich Bitch.

"Do you know," Doreen said, getting up a full head of steam, "what hassle drugs cause for the families of addicts?" She shut the door and led the way to the kitchen, sucking in Cassie's scent and pretending it was hers—it was the closest she'd get to owning any. "I told that Richie what a dramatic effect it can have, but he wouldn't listen, said a bit of pot and sniff didn't hurt no one, but it does, it can kill, and I for one think it's disgusting—and those who sell it are an' all."

That was about as close as she dared get with regards to a dig at Cassie and her old man. If she'd spelled it out, she'd have been right in the shit, so she'd have to be content with what she'd had the balls to say. Satisfaction bolstered her muscles, woke her right up, it did.

Strip-light on beneath the cupboard, kettle flicked to boil, she grabbed a pair of nude tights off the top of her washing pile on the table and used them as a dressing gown belt. It worked a treat, and she silently congratulated herself, although she might well accuse Sally of nicking hers next time she nipped round for something.

"Right then, take a pew, and let's get whatever it is said that needs to be said, then we can both go on our merry way to bed—which you got me out of, by the way. I was reading, I'll have you know, and you knocking up a storm had me jumping and I dropped the book. Now I don't know what ruddy page I was on."

"Doreen." Cassie stared at her.

Those blue eyes of hers, like one of them Mediterranean seas they were, all pure and whatnot. They gave Doreen the willies if she were honest. No kindness in them anymore, just hard steel.

Cassie pointed, her manicured red fingernail glinting. "Sit down. I'll make your tea."

Oh. It was serious then. Doreen had known that, hence the babbling, but to have it confirmed... She shuffled over and lowered her weary self onto one of the three chairs around her small pine table. The high pile of washing obscured Cassie, so Doreen shifted it over, sighing at a pair of kecks tumbling down to drape themselves on top of the radiator. She sat in silence while the kettle boiled and Cassie sorted the brew. Tense silence. The sort where you knew something terrible had happened but you didn't want to ask. If you asked, your whole world could come crashing down on you, suffocating you with its wickedness, forcing you to admit you cared for your son really, just didn't want to admit it now you'd told everyone he was a waste of space.

Tea made—only one, and Doreen inwardly sniped that Cassie probably didn't want to drink from one of *her* cups—her guest handed it over then sat opposite.

Cassie got straight to it. "Richie's been on the Barrington, selling."

She placed her hands on the table, fingers splayed, her skin so damn young Doreen had a second or two of nostalgia for the woman *she* used to be. Her hands were dry if she didn't use cream, and her veins stood up, gnarled blue tributaries the same colour as Cassie's creepy-as-fuck eyes. All those years she'd had skin like that and she hadn't appreciated it.

"I know, and like I said, it's nowt to do with me." Doreen sipped some tea, slurping it and cringing with embarrassment.

She didn't squeeze the teabag enough. It's like gnat's piss.

Cassie sighed. "He's had warnings, several, but he's ignored them."

"Do I have to say it again?" Doreen frowned. "Not. My. Business."

"Tonight was his final warning."

Those words loitered between them, as though they'd stalled midway to Doreen's ears, but shit, she'd heard them all right, loud and clear and shocking and serrated and…

"Final?" she whispered.

"I'm afraid so."

"Lenny gave the order?" Doreen's legs shook, the backs of her dangling slippers slapping on the floor where she'd pointed her toes and lifted her heels to give herself something to focus on.

Cassie didn't answer.

Anger surged. The lying bastard! Lenny had told her once upon a time he'd save Richie, and he had, yet he'd ordered the kill? "So why the fuck didn't *he* come here to tell me?" *Because of the past, because he knew he'd broken his good-for-nothing promise.* "Why did the great Lenny Grafton send *you*? You're a slip of a kid and have no right to—"

"Lenny's dead."

Doreen gaped at her. *Oh, dear God.* Two words, delivered with such sharpness, no emotion in them what-so-fucking-ever, from a girl she'd watched grow up. A whippersnapper Mam would have called her, a fucking trumped-up whippersnapper. What was *wrong* with her to not be upset at the passing of her father?

What's wrong with you to not be upset by the passing of your son?

Doreen had her reasons. She cleared her throat. "Richie knew what he was getting into so had to face any consequences." She'd said that more to herself to answer her own question, justify her non-reaction. "He stepped on Lenny's patch, sold right under his nose, and he knew he shouldn't. Several warnings, you said. Well then, he was told, and if he chose not to listen…" The last few words came out as a wail, and she clamped her stupid quivering lips closed.

"Are you okay, Doreen?"

A tiny, *tiny* glint of compassion shone in Cassie's eyes, and it almost did Doreen in.

"I'm fine. What about you?"

"Bearing up."

"How did Lenny…?"

"Heart attack."

"Oh."

Doreen sipped her tea, her jiggling legs calming down. Cassie stared at the window above the sink, but she wouldn't see much out there, the cupboard light on helping to create a reflection of the kitchen, of them, two women with people to mourn, one of them a vibrant redhead, the other older and grey beneath the blonde dye job.

"So you're running things properly now then?" Doreen sighed. "With your face being like a smacked babby's arse, I reckon you'll do well."

A slither of a smile crossed Cassie's lips, gone again in an instant.

"Did my Richie meet Marlene?" Doreen held her breath.

Cassie nodded.

"I've heard about Marlene, you know, but used to think it was some lie, something to scare the Barrington lot, that there was this woman who murdered people for Lenny. I knew different when I had need of your dad once. Disposed of him, has she?"

Another nod.

Who the hell *was* Marlene? What kind of bint killed for money? Doreen had long since believed the killer-woman lived around here, and Marlene was her undercover name or whatever.

Doreen wouldn't like to meet her in a dark alley, no matter that she'd killed her son. She'd like to thank her. Not about Richie, no, but something else. Something secret. "Ah well, I'll be selling the story that he must have gone walkabouts. You'll hear nowt to the contrary from me."

"I didn't think I would."

A change of subject was in order; Doreen didn't want to deal with her real emotions yet. "What's that perfume you've got on?"

Cassie stood. "Something Dad bought me. Look, I'm sorry, Doreen. It might not seem like it, but I am."

"Yeah, I'm sorry, too. For myself and for you, for Francis." She remained in her seat, all the bluster gone out of her. Shock tired a body out. "See yourself into the street."

Cassie walked from the kitchen, head high, spine straight, and Doreen wondered what the fuck hassle that girl would have in her future without Lenny behind her.

Life was a funny old thing, and while Doreen had vowed to cut Richie out of her feelings, she still had some, evident by the heaving sob that came out of her the second Cassie closed the front door. Doreen's boy was dead, and she'd never clip him around the earhole again.

She rested her head on the tabletop and cried.

Chapter Eleven

*L*enny got out of his car round the back of The *Mechanic's garage and stared at the van. It was black, like the caller had said, so that was one truth he'd been told. Now it was time to see if the rest was on the level. If it wasn't, he'd root out the caller somehow and clobber the bastard. What bugged him was, the caller*

had known about Jess. Why had he waited until she was dead before making contact? What had prevented him from doing so before?

Noises came from inside, the blare of the radio playing a tune from the eighties, as well as tinny banging, metal on metal, and it echoed. Annoying. Grating on Lenny's last nerve. He walked down the side of the building. What was The Mechanic doing here so late on a Sunday night? Maybe he'd had bookings and the respray on the van had taken him into overtime.

Or maybe he needed somewhere to be to keep his mind off what he'd done.

At the front, the big double doors leading to the work area stood open, letting out light, a large rectangle of it resting on the knobbly concrete forecourt, the top edge creeping up the bumper of a green Vauxhall. Book-sized white stickers with black numbers on the inside of the windscreen showed

194

prospective buyers they'd need to part with over a grand if they wanted to buy it. Other cars for sale appeared as boxy shadows, and Lenny reckoned a few might be stolen, plates changed, identification numbers filed off.

He wouldn't put it past The Mechanic, not now. Not if he'd moved on to stealing kids.

What got Lenny was he'd thought this fella was a decent sort, if a bit on the dodgy side with what he did for Lenny. He'd always done a good job valeting—as in, he got rid of any bloodstains and nefarious matter the police could be interested in, plus he provided motors if they were needed for certain schemes Lenny had on the go. He was paid handsomely to do that job, keep his mouth shut, and act to the law like he knew nowt if any questions came his way.

In short, Lenny would have said, before he'd received that phone call tonight, that The Mechanic *was one man he could trust. Now it had been said the bloke had taken Jess, everything Lenny had known had to be reordered in his brain. The Mechanic no longer occupied one of the few spots Lenny reserved for those on his good list. He was right at the bottom of the bad one, classed as lesser than pond scum, and he'd show this bloke that if you fucked with a Grafton or anyone a Grafton cared about, you were dead.*

He'd thought beyond killing him. The disposal was something he'd enjoy later. An idea had come years ago, along with the clarity he always experienced after a murder, as if his mind cleared of everything except what he had to do to conceal it. He'd had a piece of machinery modified which now suited his murderous needs, suited the size of bodies. Marlene, he'd called it, but only a handful of people knew she was an inanimate object and not a woman.

The song in the garage changed to I'll be Missing You *by Puff Daddy and Faith Evans, and it got Lenny right in the heart. Joe and Lou would be missing little Jess for the rest of their lives, theirs destroyed by The Mechanic's need to abduct then kill.*

Shit didn't add up, though. The Mechanic wasn't a killer, Lenny would never have pegged him as such. Or maybe he was but he'd hidden it all these years. Some folks were dark like that, weren't they, thinking shit, imagining it, keeping it hidden because they knew it was wrong, even if it didn't feel that way to them. The Mechanic's love for his wife was well-known, how devoted he was to her, how they'd been trying for so long to have kids.

So why snatch one? Kill one?

It had to be a blessing they didn't have any of their own. Who knew if he'd have killed them an' all? Fucking scaggy ponce.

Even more riled up, Lenny entered the garage and checked where the bastard was. Down there in the pit, beneath a car, smacking the shit out of the undercarriage using an iron bar. Lenny closed the double doors, slid the bolts across, then moved over to the radio sitting on a wooden bench that ran halfway along the right-hand side.

He switched it off.

The clanging stopped.

"Who's there?" The Mechanic called.

Lenny counted to five to up the tension. "Me."

"Ay up, Lenny. What brings you here?"

Lenny frowned. The man had sounded normal, his usual jovial self. Had the caller given false information? Had The Mechanic pissed them off so they wanted revenge, grassing him up for something he hadn't done?

The black van, though.

"I need you to clarify something for me," Lenny said.

The Mechanic clambered out of the pit and dusted off his boilersuit. A Tetris block slotting into place in Lenny's mind, he came to the realisation the second piece of the puzzle was right there. The boilersuit was navy, the same as the one the abductor had on, and he should have twigged back then that he'd seen it many times before when he'd dropped his vehicles here.

But no one would suspect The Mechanic, the happy-go-lucky garage owner, therefore, Lenny hadn't either.

"Nice outfit." Lenny nodded to it.

"Eh?" The Mechanic frowned. "Same as I've always got on."

"Open that filing cabinet." Lenny gestured that way.

The Mechanic laughed, the burble of it unsteady. "What?"

"Open it."

"Why?"

Lenny's temper flared. He wasn't used to people questioning him, not these days, not now he ran the Barrington and everyone knew it. 'What Lenny says goes' was a mantra around here, one people would do best to heed. People like this ponce here.

"Just open it." Lenny took a gun out of his jacket pocket and aimed it. "As you can see, I'm not fucking about, pal."

The Mechanic gave him a wary glance, walked over to the cabinet, and stood in front of it, head bent. He was side-on, so Lenny couldn't see all of his expression, but one cheek flared red, a signal of guilt if ever there was one. The man had done wrong, was working out what he could do to smooth things over.

"If you're not going to do as you're told, how about you tell me why you snatched Jess Wilson." Lenny stared at him, his heartbeat tripping over itself. Fuck, his chest was tight, an invisible band compressing it, always happening when adrenaline sped through him.

The Mechanic hung his head even more. "Pack it in, Lenny."

"You should know me by now. I don't pack anything in until I've got the information I'm after. Open the bastard cabinet."

The Mechanic reached out and opened the door, the contents displayed good and proper. The shotgun stood on its end, the other pointing upwards. A balled-up boilersuit sat on the bottom, and a black scribble of wool perched on top, the same sort as a balaclava. If he had owt about him, The Mechanic could reach in and grab that shotgun, fire it at Lenny, but he stood there, gazing at it.

"Why?" Lenny asked.

A shoulder slump. "For the ransom money. You were meant to shell out for her."

All this was over money? "I didn't get a note."

"I posted it. It'll probably arrive tomorrow."

"What did you need the money for?"

The Mechanic sighed. "Private IVF. We've used up all our chances with the NHS."

"I would've helped. The community would've helped. Karen would've written an article, sent it out for donations. We'd have raised money, you fucking well know that." *A pause.* "Where did you keep her?"

"At my place."

"You what? Did Alisha know? Did your wife have anything to do with this?" *If she did, God bloody help her.*

The Mechanic shook his head. "Fuck no. I'd never involve her with anything illegal."

"Yet she knows what you do for me, with the cars. That's being involved. Where's she been, your missus, to not know a kid's in her house?"

The Mechanic jerked up one shoulder. "I drugged the girl. Put her in the spare room. I use it as my office. Alisha never goes in there."

The idea of that screwed with Lenny's brain. Drugged? He'd drugged a kiddie? Put her in an office all by herself? "Why is she dead?"

The Mechanic closed the cabinet door and turned to glare at Lenny. "I didn't do that. Don't you fucking put me in the frame for it. She got out while I was...was busy. Alisha was out shopping. That babby left my house off her own back, wandered somewhere, she must have done, because there's no way I'd have killed her. I just wanted money so Alisha got what she wanted. I was going to take Jess back to the farm."

Lenny didn't even bother laughing wryly. He was too arsey for that. Too appalled. "And I'm meant to believe that?"

Another insolent jerk of the shoulder. "Well, yeah, because it's the truth."

"Bollocks." Lenny jabbed his head to the side. "Out."

The Mechanic did as he was told, walking over to open one of the doors. He stepped outside, and Lenny expected him to bolt, but The Mechanic waited, clearly knowing that what would happen next was inevitable. Clearly knowing if he legged it, Lenny would go after Alisha.

"Go round the back. I'm parked there," Lenny ordered.

The Mechanic went down the side of the building, and Lenny kept close in case the fella did have a mind to run. He didn't, he slowed if anything, and at Lenny's car, he waited by the boot. Yeah, he knew what came next. He'd cleaned enough of Lenny's boots to know it'd have his blood in it soon an' all.

What a pisser. Lenny would have to find another trustworthy valet or do it himself in future.

He popped it open, and The Mechanic climbed in, curling himself into the foetal position, hugging his knees like some little boy. Lenny pistol-whipped him in the temple and kept doing it despite the man's shouts, until the fucker was out of it, eyes closed, blood oozing and dripping, flesh expanding in that puffy way it had when damaged.

He closed the lid and got in the driver's seat, placing his shooter in a carrier bag from the glove box. No need to dirty up the interior upholstery, was there. He drove around aimlessly, working out where to dump the remains of the body. It'd be fitting if it was on Joe Wilson's land, a grave dug on the outskirts in a faraway field, but with the police still sniffing around, that option was closed to him.

Lenny thought of the blood spatter created by a gunshot wound. Normally, he shot people out in the open, in the woods, marching his captives there under the cover of darkness, but there was another place where blood was the norm, and he didn't know why he hadn't thought of it before—why he hadn't thought of introducing The Mechanic to Marlene while he was still alive. Now he came to think of it, it was the perfect cover. No one would hear his screams in the meat factory.

He drove there, parking round the back, and opened the door, the one the deliveries came through. A short corridor led to the storage area, then beyond was the machinery room, and off to the side was a room containing Marlene.

The mincer.

He nodded and went back outside, his plan fully formed. He'd ordered a new mincer a few years ago, had the current one placed in the side room, and in the middle of the night, men had come to add a chute on top and steps leading up to it. He'd claimed the mincer was broken, that'd kept the workers from asking questions, and only the trusted had a key to the room and were allowed to use Marlene.

He collected his gun from the carrier bag and slid it into his waistband. Hauled The Mechanic from the boot and dragged him through to the side room, dumping him on the floor. He moved to Marlene and stroked her flank. To show people on the Barrington he meant business more than usual, he'd soon put out a rumour that he'd hired some woman to kill people for him, and everyone would know when they heard her name they were destined for death.

He caressed the cold steel. "Marlene has always had a nice ring to it." He chuckled and imagined the future: "If you don't do what he wants, he'll take you to Marlene."

A roar of laughter pealed out of him, and he fired the old girl up, his partner in crime, one who wouldn't open her gob and grass on him, because after every human had been fed through her, she'd be cleaned, all evidence removed, the room locked up tight.

Perfect. Fucking perfect.

The Mechanic stirred. Lenny kicked him awake, and the fear in the bloke's eyes was like nowt else. Lenny reckoned it was the whir Marlene was giving off, that menacing grumble she belted out as if her inner teeth were grinding in anticipation of meat and bones.

"Please, no," The Mechanic wailed.

"Oh, give over, you wet wanker." Lenny grabbed him beneath the armpits and propped him on his feet. He whipped his gun out. "Get undressed."

Despite the terror of this situation, The Mechanic laughed. Nerves, most likely. "You what?"

"Get undressed."

Lenny's prey did what was asked of him, embarrassed, his cheeks turning a shade of red, the raspberry ripple in ice cream. Naked, he cupped his crown jewels, and far from setting Lenny off laughing, it fucking annoyed him. After all The Mechanic had done, he still clung to his modesty. After kidnapping a little girl, drugging her, murdering her, dumping her by The Beast, he was bothered about his baggy nuts and shrivelled-with-fear dick.

Lenny poked his gun towards Marlene. "Get in." He aimed the shooter at the scum in front of him, waving it to get his point fully across. "Get. In."

The Mechanic swallowed, that larynx of his having a good old boing, a Golden Delicious in a game of bobbing apples. His throat must be dry with dread. Regardless, he climbed up the steps to the human-wide chute and managed to balance on the edge of the round opening facing Lenny, his legs drawn up beneath him in a squat, probably because he had no idea how far down Marlene's teeth were and didn't want her to chomp on his toes.

Lenny tilted his head. Stared. "Lie down."

The Mechanic shook his head, banging it on the side of the chute. "No, please, no. I swear to God, I didn't kill her."

"You're lying. You took her, jabbed a shotgun in her father's face, and you drove away with her. Who's the bloke in the back of the van?"

"Fuck off."

"Stretch. Those. Legs. Out." Lenny cocked the trigger.

As if a bullet to the head was worse than being gnawed to death, The Mechanic did as instructed. Maybe the silent threat to Alisha had returned. Lenny would do the same to save Francis, so they had something in common, even this far down the evil road.

He pushed on the man's head, waiting for the scream when the blades sliced at his feet. It came, loud and wretched, right from his damned and pockmarked soul, and Lenny pushed some more, feeding the legs into Marlene's throat, then his pelvis. Blood gushed out of the wanker's gob, some spraying onto Lenny's shirt, his suit, but he kept pressing against the resistance of the chopping blades, Marlene maybe struggling with the bones like she sometimes did. Then she sucked the man in, the torso something she liked the best, greedy to have it in her grumbling belly.

Lenny glanced at the large collection bin. Mince spewed out of Marlene, a super-thick sausage, pink and red and white, bits breaking off, the clumps landing with damp thuds.

The Mechanic stopped screaming, his lips parted in a skewed circle, his teeth bared, those and his gums stained scarlet. The rest of him slid down the chute with another shove from Lenny, the hands the last thing to disappear into the blackness of the tube.

"Fucking child-killing cunt."

Blood smears marred the opening of the chute, nice and crimson, the sign of a job well done.

Lenny left Marlene to run for a minute or so then switched her off.

The silence calmed his racing mind.

He had work to do, getting the bits of person mince out of her, then he'd have to take the plastic container with mince and dispose of it.

His earlier thought of taking this bastard to Handel Farm sprang back into his head, and he smiled.

Joe kept pigs. Lots of them.

They'd be having a feast tonight.

Chapter Twelve

The Barrington Life - Your Weekly

SEARCH FOR THE KILLER CONTINUES!

Karen Scholes - All Things Crime in our Time
Sharon Barnett - Chief Editor

EVENING SPECIAL. MONDAY JUNE 30th 1997

Just a reminder about the money for the horse-and-carriage hearse. I've only had fifty quid donated, and that's a piss-poor show in my opinion. Come on, if we all gave a quid, we'd have enough, considering how many of us live on the estate. A pound. That's all. Go without in aid of a good cause. Wouldn't you want people to do that for your child? How cruel to ignore our angel like this, as if she doesn't matter. Money. Drop it off. Now.

I've been and given my official statement to the police, and word has it they're no closer to finding the killer than they were before. Honestly, if they weren't so busy trying to catch speeding motorists and the like with those stupid hand-held cameras, hiding in bushes and shit, they'd do a damn sight better job in finding Jess's killer.

In other worrying news, The Mechanic, our very own Dave Colson, has gone missing. As of last night, apparently. Alisha has phoned the police, but of course, they gave the usual codswallop about him needing to be gone for forty-eight hours. Keep your eye out for him, will you? It's not like him to sod off, is it, he's devoted to Alisha, and he had bookings today for tuning engines and whatnot so wouldn't let anyone down on purpose. He's a good bloke is our Dave.

What's the world coming to, eh? Jess, Dave, it's all a bit much to be honest.

If anyone wants to send flowers for Jess's funeral, don't. Joe and Lou Wilson would like the money spent on your own kiddies instead. Joe asked me to pass this on: "Treat them, love them while you've got them, because one day they might be gone."

I couldn't have said it better myself. My cousin let her kids stay up late watching telly last night with a big bag of sweets, and they thought it was Christmas. Look after each other, yeah? Care for your fellow neighbour. I know we don't all get on, but in times like these, a small smile won't hurt you.

And remember to drop that bloody hearse money round or I'll set Lenny on you. Failing that, I'll punch your lights out. By the way, I'm excluded from caring for my fellow neighbour, obviously.

Joke.

Chapter Thirteen

B eing on the Barrington after so many years was strange yet at the same time the perfect homecoming. There was a bit called New Barrington now, built in his absence, massive houses on the other side of Sculptor's Field. Of course, his mother had told him about it on the phone, as she had with all the changes around here. The last time he'd visited Sculptor's was when Jessica Wilson had been dumped beside The Beast.

He'd left the following week for work, landed himself a job with a firm based in Newcastle, but he was back now, in the place he knew best. He'd come home to die, his aching chest turning into pains, and his heart was too damaged to fix. It'd be ages before a match came up to replace it, and he'd been warned he didn't have long left. He was old anyroad, so it was inevitable he'd leave this earth soon.

He'd dreamt about it, coming here, the night-time films in his head full of friends, family, and the scenery he was so familiar with. He remembered his life here, how the sometimes fractured community came together in a crisis as if they'd never had a cross word spoken between them. How folks were always on hand to lend you a fiver or treat you to a night in The Donny if times were hard. You couldn't beat that, the feeling of belonging.

Towards the end of his years away, his nomadic life on the road as a haulage driver had left him unsettled, missing something, probably the place he'd called home. He'd never felt the same about Newcastle, although those on his estate were nice enough. But they weren't the Barrington lot, and he'd missed the bonhomie — and the spats, which were always good to witness.

Full circle by being here then, where he'd been born, although he *had* nipped back for his mother's funeral, disappearing again straight after. He'd only attended to make sure she was really dead. She was someone he hadn't missed but had kept in touch with her so she'd pass on the news. He had to keep abreast of what was going on.

He stood in on the imaginary line that split New Barrington from Old and stared at The Beast, still the same creepy white thing he remembered. That had featured in his dreams an' all, and there was nowt he could do to stop it. In the nightmares it starred in, it came alive, stone limbs loosening, head going up and down, tail swishing, and it chased him all over the estate until he reached Lenny Grafton's doorstep and fell in a heap. It was like it forced him there, delivering him to the gangster.

It wasn't lost on him, the meaning of it.

Chapter Fourteen

On this cold and blustery January day, their quiet Christmas a distant memory, one Cassie would rather forget, a mass of mourners stood around the rectangular hole in the ground two weeks after Lenny's death. Most Cassie knew, but some were strangers. She couldn't help but wonder whether they'd come to gawp from other areas in Nottinghamshire, some as far as Yorkshire and Lincoln, to mix with those who'd run with a renowned gangster, making them important by association—and to see how she coped with the funeral.

In their eyes, her reactions would prove what sort of woman she was, but she couldn't win however she acted. If she kept the tears at bay like Mam wanted, she'd be deemed hard, unfeeling, a right little cow, but if she cried, well, she'd be soft, someone they couldn't trust to rule the estate.

She'd opted for allowing her eyes to fill but not let the tears fall. If anyone watched, they'd see she'd loved her father but she was strong and could cope even in this harrowing situation. Via Mam, she now paid a lot of their wages, the drug runners, the sex worker handlers, the mob hands, the meat factory employees to name but a few.

And while the high-rises technically belonged to Mam, along with a few houses, Cassie was the landlord to every single resident in those flats, and if they reneged on their tenancy agreement, they had one warning from the heavies, then Cassie would give the word to evict them—the illegal way. No court orders, none of that tenants' rights shit, they were gone, ousted under the cover of darkness, the neighbours wondering if they'd done a moonlight or if they'd been forced to go.

Only one family had got that far with Lenny in charge, and it had been enough of a warning for no one else to opt for non-payment of rent. She hoped it wouldn't come to that, her having to make a show of being as ruthless as her father. Still, she was prepared to do it all in his memory, and anyone who didn't like it could go and fuck themselves with a sharp stick.

Mam, stoic and in control of herself, stood to Cassie's right, Jason to her left. He'd been surprisingly tender since Dad's death, foregoing his usual nosy manner for someone who presented himself as a friend, a shoulder to lean on (because she'd never cry on it). She'd asked herself last week whether she'd now consider his offer of seeing him outside work, starting slow like he'd said, seeing if there was more than a working relationship to be had.

She was still undecided.

The vicar droned on, his voice a boring monotone, the wind lashing at his jowly cheeks, sending them red and mottled, his white outfit pushed to one side, the hem rippling. Cassie tuned him out, going into her gangster role of scoping the attendees and checking for danger,

Dad's voice urging her to do it. As she'd had the job passed down to her, who knew whether anyone would try to kill her, taking the title that way. Men stood close by, guns concealed beneath their calf-length black cashmere coats. Spotters, Lenny had dubbed them, people who kept watch and protected him.

Now they were here for her and Mam.

Trevor and Lisa Bayliss huddled together on the other side of the grave, heads bowed, Lisa's arm through the crook of her husband's. They appeared genuinely sad, or maybe it was the prospect of working for Cassie that had them so glum.

Poor Brenda sobbed noisily, a wrinkled tissue permanently beneath her reddened nose. She'd been fond of Dad then, more than Cassie had realised. Then there was Joe and Lou, him absolutely gutted, face pale, her as skinny as always, glancing at Cassie every so often, maybe wondering what Jess would have looked like at her age.

So many emotions and feelings must be going through those gathered, a funeral sparking memories of others they'd attended, people crying not only for Lenny Grafton but their own dearly departed relatives, scabs picked, open wounds once again, the blood flowing along with the vicar's words.

Felix and Ted, old soldiers in this game of gangsters, stood close together, the tops of their black-sleeved arms touching, grey-haired heads bent as they paid their respects. It must be hard for them, having worked for Dad since he'd bought the meat factory, running the Saturday market stall for him, drugs passed over with the lamb chops, the pork loins, baggies of cocaine concealed in lumps of mince. The food with drugs in them had blue tape at the top of the bags to keep them closed, the normal stuff yellow.

Doreen leant against Harry Benson, him as slender as a lamppost, and it had even been said he was much like a streetlamp, lighting her path. Someone had actually used that analogy, Cassie couldn't recall who it was, after news had spread that Richie had fucked off without a by your leave, not even telling his mam where he was going. He'd been cursed up one street and down another. Doreen had gone round to his bedsit to collect a few things, personal stuff he wouldn't want anyone nosing at, and came out to declare someone had raided his bedsit, stealing his bike battery and the safe containing drugs and money.

Gossip burnt through the Barrington, a wildfire, speculation rife as to who'd done such a thing, but no one had come forward to claim that the money and gear belonged to them. Cassie wasn't surprised. It'd mean them admitting they'd sent Richie out to peddle for them, and Cassie would have them dealt with.

You didn't step forward so someone could kill you, did you.

Mam gasped, bringing Cassie out of her head and back to the funeral, to the expensive box which had been lowered into the ground while she'd drifted off. Mam bent to grasp some soil and throw it in, and the crackle-thwap of it hitting the coffin lid gave Cassie a jolt. She was next to do the same, the mud cold even through her gloves, a heavy clump she hadn't expected to hold until she was in her forties. She tossed it in, said a silent goodbye, and vowed she'd do her father proud. She'd look after Mam, run both sides of the business, and ensure no one messed her or anyone else around. If they did, they'd have her to contend with, a harder version of their previous leader—they'd discover that soon enough.

Cassie stepped back, zoning out again, thinking about the previous fortnight where she'd visited everyone involved under her direction, Jason by her side. She'd dropped in on all employees, tenants, and residents, too, letting them know she was the one they answered to now, as if that was in any doubt, and made no bones about the consequences if they fucked her around.

New rules established, she'd asked herself which one of them would try her, push her, test her limits. Someone would, it was the way of things, but it would only take that one person's punishment to show the others who was boss.

Cassie Grafton.

Mourners drifted away with the last words falling from the vicar's mouth, off to The Donny for the wake. Mam was swallowed up in a sea of people wanting to offer her some comfort, and she smiled and nodded despite the grief that must be burning her up inside. Jason wandered off to speak with Felix and Ted, Cassie standing there alone for a blissful few seconds until Doreen left Harry to come and stand in front of her.

"Probably not the place to say it, duck, but thanks for the perfume." Doreen smiled, her lips wobbling. "Found it on my doorstep the day after you came about Richie, I did. Once I gave it a whiff, I knew it was from you. I'd have kept my mouth shut regardless."

"It wasn't a bribe, Doreen."

"Oh."

"You knew the score already, there was no need for me to pile it on. The perfume was a gift."

"Right. I don't get gifts if it isn't Christmas or my birthday." Doreen gazed around, her eyes darting. She leant closer and whispered, "Is that Marlene woman here?"

Cassie made a show of looking for her. "She was, but she must have gone."

"Oh. I did wonder if it was the tart in the big sunglasses. I mean, you don't wear them on dark days like this, do you, so I thought she might be hiding behind them."

"Maybe she didn't want anyone to see her puffy eyes. She was good to Dad. Never let him down."

"Yes, that must be it. I have to say, in normal circumstances I would've gone right up to her and asked her how she"—Doreen cast her gaze about again—"killed my son, what she did to him, but, you know, with my promise to keep schtum, and you right there ready to take me out if I even dared…" She shrugged. "It was an urge, didn't last long, and won't happen again. I wanted to be honest with you, tell you how I was feeling, like."

"Make sure it *doesn't* happen again." Cassie had been thinking of Doreen ever since she'd nipped round to give her the news. Like her father would have done, she'd examined ways she could further keep Doreen in her pocket, and today was as good a time as any to put forward what she'd devised. "Come with me a second."

Cassie guided her between other graves to the path that wound off to the left over to the car park. People got into their cars, the promise of a free bar and buffet undoubtedly on their minds, time to reminisce about Lenny Grafton and all the

232

things he'd got up to. She stopped by the final resting place of one Gertrude Noble, ninety-six, beloved mother of Maurice and Carol, friend to many, loved forever.

Doreen stared at her, worry stitched into every wrinkle on her face, drawing them tight. "What did I do? Am I in bother?"

Cassie laid a hand on the woman's shoulder. "No. I want to offer you a job."

Doreen's lips parted, her lower teeth revealed, her chin turning into two. "Eh? But I've *got* a job. I love the betting shop, wouldn't want to leave old Fredrick in the lurch. He's getting on a bit and relies on me so he can have a break."

"You'd still work there, but I want you to be my ears."

Doreen's eyes filled. "Your ears? That's a big job, that is. And what about Karen and Sharon? Aren't they the ears?"

"They are, and they still will be, but they're Lenny's ears, and I want my own, someone who won't keep shit from me because they watched me grow up and think I'm still that little girl. You know I'm not her anymore, how I was when I came to your place. I want someone for myself— one who'll also keep an eye on Karen and Sharon." Cassie paused to think on whether she could divulge her real fear. "Are you in or not?"

"Do I have a choice?"

"Yes."

"Okay, then I'll do it. How much?"

"Five hundred a week whether you hear anything or not."

"Bloody Nora. Is that what Karen and Sharon get?"

"Yes."

"But they sort *The Life*. They walk all over the Barrington each week to deliver it."

"Along with a few kids—it's not all down to them, much as Karen would like you to believe that." Cassie leant closer. "I'm going to tell you something, and you keep it to yourself, got it?"

Doreen nodded.

"Karen and Sharon, they're nice enough, but I've always had the feeling they think *they* run the Barrington to an extent. They're the eyes and ears, yes, they pass on information, they get the community spirit going—well, Karen does, she's the one who writes the articles—but I don't want them thinking, because Dad's gone, that they can step up their game, if you see what I mean, try to take over in a way. I've been to visit them, like I have with everyone else who works for me now,

235

and they assured me they wouldn't step on toes, but part of me doesn't believe that."

"I getcha." Doreen nodded. Her attention strayed to the women in question, who clucked around Mam.

Cassie visualised them twittering in Mam's ear, trying to gauge if they'd heard right, from Cassie's own lips, that they had to obey her now. "Surely you're in charge behind the scenes, Francis…" and "Do we really have to listen to her?" Or maybe Cassie had imagined the unseen bristles chafing her when she'd gone to see them. Maybe the two women were fine with her dishing out orders. After all, she'd been helping Dad for ages before his death.

But they could have tolerated me for him.

"So I'll listen out for gossip then," Doreen said. "Perhaps offer my services to help deliver *The Life*. Get in with them."

Cassie had made the right choice. Doreen had got the gist without her having to say it outright.

"That's exactly what I want you to do, Doreen. Make new friends as it were—or rekindle old friendships. Mam said you didn't get on with Karen very well anymore."

"Right. I can do that, and as for Karen, that spat we had was years ago, so she needs to get over herself if she still holds a grudge."

"No one but us can know." Cassie gave her a tight smile. "Only Mam."

"Of course. Do you think I want you carting me off to Marlene? Good grief, duck, she's not someone I want to meet."

Cassie dipped a hand in her bag and brought out a cheap smartphone. She switched it on and showed Doreen the contact list. Only one name in it.

The Boss.

"Contact me on this. If you text, you have to write 'news' for general things. If it's urgent, you write 'problem'. Anything else, life-or-death shit, you ring me—but only in those circumstances."

Doreen took the phone, then the charger Cassie handed over. "How do I get paid?"

"Cash. I'll bring it round to yours every week, Monday nights after ten. Best if Harry's scarce, either at his own house or asleep in your bed. Your role is a secret. If I put it through the letterbox, he might ask what it is."

"Someone's going to spot that red hair of yours at my door."

Cassie smiled wider. "No they won't. I'll be in disguise."

Chapter Fifteen

Jason drove towards The Donny, anger filling him until he reckoned it'd burst out and he'd mow down the next person who had a mind to step into the road in front of his car. It'd serve them right for chancing it, trying to get from one side to the other while he sped along, and he'd claim it was an accident: "They walked right out in front of me, nowt I could do to stop it."

God, he needed to kill someone so badly. Since he'd offed Richie Prince, the urge to do it again had prodded at him, a constant poking finger, but he'd held the desire inside, imagining it instead each night in bed, eyes closed, guts and blood spilling from whoever he'd stabbed, his insane laughter so real he'd been brought up short to realise he'd actually been doing it, wetting himself, worrying Mam would come in from her room next door and ask him what he was playing at. "Waking me at two in the morning, lad, you daft get."

Also, he was sick to the back teeth of acting, doing it Brenda's way, and it had only been a relatively short while of taking her advice. He'd since made a firmer plan, one he'd see play out soon, and if Cassie didn't make a move with regards to them seeing one another outside the job, he'd push a bit harder on that front.

He wanted the money, the notoriety, couldn't get it fast enough.

Things had been going well, he'd admit that, although it pissed him off Brenda was right on that score. Cassie had confided a few things to him since he'd pulled back on being nosy—not about the business, more's the pity—to do with Lenny and how she felt about him. Jason supposed that was something. She rarely opened up, so for him to be the one she shared her emotions with must count for something. Plus, Lenny had paired them together, so surely she realised Jason was the best one to shadow her. If Lenny had arranged it, it must be so.

"Your dad wanted us as a team," he'd said. "And we'll make a good one, the best. I'll stick by your side and protect you. He knew I would, he told me as much."

Bullshit, but whatever. Lenny wasn't around to dispute Jason's lies.

The night he'd got home after taking the safe from Richie's flat, he'd gone on a bender with the white stuff once Mam was in bed. He'd sniffed it so far up his nose it had stung something rotten, his eyes watering. He'd livened right up, relived Richie's murder in his head, but on the comedown, he'd remembered why he'd killed him instead of giving him another verbal warning.

'I know you of old, remember, and you were a prick when we were kids, so why the hell should I do as you tell me since you're still a prick now?'

Fucking little bastard.

Of course, the memories had come out to bug him then, tormenting him, his father's mouth

242

opening to spew the very word Jason hated so much when it was directed at him. *'Prick. You're a prick, son.'* Jason didn't know why his dad hated him so much, why he'd treated Mam with no respect. He was from Yorkshire and said he was made of stern stuff, didn't suffer fools gladly, but for Pete's sake, you were meant to love your wife and kid, weren't you?

Colin Shepherd was a mean bastard in his time, no other word for him, and Mam, no matter how much she acted like she was better than everyone else on the Barrington, couldn't hide the bruises if they were on her face. Until he'd gone to school and found out otherwise, Jason thought all mams had them, the blues and plums, the mustards and greens, the busted lips, and eyes where the whites were sometimes red, veins prominent. It wasn't until he'd asked a pal why *their* mam didn't look like his sometimes that he discovered things weren't right.

"So doesn't your dad wallop your mammy then?" he'd asked, confused, his stomach hurting like it always did when he thought of his father.

"Nah, only me when I'm naughty."

Had Jason inherited his dad's need to hurt people? Was it in his blood, his genes? Or was it because he'd watched beatings from an early age and his brain thought it was a normal thing to do, even though he knew deep in his soul it wasn't? The thing was, as a kid he'd imagined punching and kicking folks, going up to them if they pissed him off and decking them. Going up to them if they *hadn't* pissed him off, just starting on them for no reason. He'd had to hold it in, telling himself he couldn't become *that* person.

And then his world had changed. Jason had bumped into Lenny one day, who'd strutted out of The Donny as if he owned the place, and Jason had wanted to be exactly like him.

"Ay up, lad," Lenny had said. "What's the mizzy face all about then? Come on, tell Uncle Lenny all about it."

Uncle Lenny. That had lightened Jason's heart.

They'd walked through Old Barrington, chatting. By the time they'd got to Jason's embarrassing street, he'd agreed to sell drugs and become one of Lenny's regular peddlers, the idea sold to him with the promise of money in his pocket, notoriety amongst his peers, but the main draw: Colin Shepherd would be dealt with.

Jason didn't know why he'd spilt it all to Lenny, why he'd opened up and let someone outside their home know what Dad got up to, but he had, and Lenny's promise had been the best thing Jason had ever heard.

"My friend Marlene will sort things," Lenny had said upon hearing of Jason's upbringing and how Mam had suffered. His face had clouded, like someone should have told him what Mam had gone through before then, how his spies hadn't passed on the information.

How they'd failed her.

Lenny's exit from The Donny had stuck in Jason's head all this time. How the man had commanded the very air around him, how his assured walk and hefty figure meant you shut up and listened, you walked home with him, you called him Uncle Lenny. Jason had fashioned himself on him, acting the same, giving off the aura that had no name but had people giving you a wide berth. Then and there, he'd told himself *he'd* run the Barrington one day, *he'd* swagger from The Donny and scare people shitless. *He'd* live Lenny's high life.

He hadn't expected it to come so soon, though. Hadn't expected Lenny to die yet. Jason had planned to get in with Cassie first, move into her flat above the garage on the New Barrington gaff, become a proper part of the family, not just Lenny's surrogate son. Then, when Lenny died years later, he'd have done all the groundwork with Cassie already and would become the new version of Lenny Grafton.

Instead, Lenny had died early, and Cassie had the top spot, that Francis woman probably guiding her in the background, but that was okay, Jason still had time. He'd get that house on New Barrington for Mam if it was the last thing he did. She'd live right next door to him.

He sighed and parked round the back of The Donny, switching the engine off and waiting for a minute or two. Anger burned brighter—

247

thinking about his dad did that to him—and he needed to calm down, present a placid front to Cassie. And to Francis, who'd been eyeing him lately like she knew exactly what he was up to, the canny bitch. He supposed she'd seen all sorts, all walks of life, all personalities during Lenny's reign and could spot a devious bastard a mile away.

Odd how Lenny hadn't copped on to Jason's real motives.

Or maybe he had and was playing the game of keeping his enemies closer.

Jason got out of his little runner, naffed now he thought about it, that he hadn't been in the funeral car with Cassie and Francis. He'd thought he'd be by Cassie's side throughout today, not relegated to being a no-mark who wasn't classed as family when Lenny had given him the impression he was. Well, mother and daughter would pay for that one day when he snatched the crown. He'd find out who was on his side and ask the most eager to deal with Cassie and her mam—once he had a wedding ring on his finger and had ingrained himself so far into the business he knew it like the back of his Veeted hand. (He didn't do body hair, it reminded him of his father. Every five weeks, he got waxed all over apart from his eyebrows and hair.)

He walked round to the front of the pub wondering whether Cassie liked manscaped men.

Muffled laughter filtered out through the closed windows, the shapes of people filling the pub visible through the panes, the booths chocka with mourners, the bar propped up, the stage set with the karaoke equipment, something Lenny would have wanted. Jason pushed inside, the sense of being swallowed up engulfing him, and not in a good way. Most people who walked into a mass of folks they'd grown up knowing would have the feeling of coming home, of being with the people who had your back, but he'd always been an outsider, even though those looking in would consider him an important part of the Grafton gangster machine.

He didn't feel like he'd come home at all, more like he was a maggot surrounded by a murder of crows waiting to peck him to death.

That didn't sit well. He wanted to belong, wanted so badly to *be* someone, yet his childhood and how he'd been treated would always play a part, his self-confidence a wreck underneath all the bluster, the veneer he'd created that had those on the Barrington thinking he had his shit together.

Webs. People weaved them to disguise so many things, and he was the biggest spider of them all.

One day, once he'd reached his goal, he might finally be at peace with who he was.

One day, he wouldn't believe he was that prick Colin Shepherd had called him.

The teachings of the father ran deep.

He fixed a respectful smile in place at the greetings from the mourners and headed straight for Cassie, who stood by herself in the corner by the buffet table, observing in her usual way. She was rarely off the clock, always on her guard, apart from the couple of times she'd lowered it to allow him in. Brenda went up to her and bent her head to talk. Probably some business, another old fella to fleece.

You'd think she'd have left that for today.

Jason pushed through the crowd, ignoring the shit-stained glare from Francis, and joined Cassie and Brenda. Cassie gave him one of her tight smiles, the sort that had no warmth in it and passed as her version of being pleased to see him—she was such an odd duck now, so steely and hard.

"Everything okay?" He looked from Cassie to Brenda.

"I was just saying I need to go," Brenda said. "I don't like to cut it short, especially because of what today is, but as Lenny would say, business is business, and it comes before pleasure. Not that this is a pleasure; the wake, I mean."

"I know what you're saying." Cassie patted Brenda's shoulder. "I'm sorry work came up."

"When you texted me just now, I knew it'd be something like that." Brenda smiled. "Right, I'm off then. I'll nip home and get my documents, then go and introduce myself to him. I wonder if he'll recognise me."

Hmm, so there *was* a new mark to steal life savings from, and yeah, Lenny would have sent her off to do her thing despite being at a fucking wake. Even the dead didn't matter if there was work to be done, money to be made. It annoyed Jason how everyone still acted like Lenny ran the place, how his ghost—or his devil, depending which side of the fence you sat on—directed what happened. Cassie had told him recently she'd do everything in his honour, and when Jason had suggested she forged her own path, move with the times, she'd glared at him so hard, then reminded him she'd changed the rules about verbal warnings. There was only one now, then Marlene got to work.

"So I *have* forged my own path," she'd said.

He'd been momentarily scared of her, and she'd gone inside herself as if inspecting her thoughts.

Not knowing what went on in that woman's head unnerved him.

Brenda flounced off, and Cassie took a mini sausage roll off a nearby plate and bit into it.

"Who's the fella?" Jason asked—he was entitled to as her right hand. If he had to keep her safe, he had to know stuff. Not than an old man posed a threat, but still, that was what Jason told himself.

"One of those weird coincidences. It's some bloke Brenda already knows. He moved away years ago but has come back to die. She'll tell him during the time he was away she became a nurse. Some bullshit. This one will be easy. She had a fling with him. Brenda's younger than him and fancied an older bloke back then—he might still be flattered that she wants to do the same again."

"Saves her laying the groundwork then, reeling him in."

"Yep."

"You didn't say who he was," he reminded her, eager to know everything.

"I know." She picked up a cocktail stick with cheese and pineapple on the end. Bit the cheddar off. Chewed.

Fuck. Why didn't she share certain information with him? He was her *right hand*, for shit's sake, he should be in the know, yet she insisted on keeping things to herself. Brenda wouldn't open her gob, so he was out of luck there. It wouldn't do any good to question her handler either, that Trevor, and as for his missus, Lisa, she wouldn't spill owt.

Jason was the equivalent of a car stuck in a lay-by while all the other vehicles sped past on the road. No matter what his title, what his status, he wasn't really in that inner circle.

It rankled.

"Do you need a drink or owt?" he asked.

"No, thanks."

Cassie ate the pineapple, dropped the cocktail stick in a bin beneath the table, and walked off into the melee, doing her duty, as always. If it didn't look weird and bring up questions later, he'd go and follow Brenda, wait outside her house while she got the documents, then tail her to the mark's house, but it *would* look weird, and he couldn't afford to set Cassie's radar off.

Francis stared over Doreen's shoulder at him, and once again he got the uncomfortable feeling she had his measure. Well, he'd just have to put his acting head on and get her to think different.

He didn't need her sticking her oar in. So he smiled at her, nodded, and turned to place a hand on Ted's back, sidling close to listen in on their chatter, see if *they* let anything slip.

He'd get well in with Felix and his cousin, Ted. Find out as much as he could. If they didn't let him in on shit, one night, when a body needed mincing, he'd hide outside the meat factory and film them going in with a body and leaving with mince.

He cursed himself for not thinking of ensuring he had insurance before.

'That's because you're an incompetent prick, son.'

Chapter Sixteen

Brenda parked outside Vance Johnson's bungalow, the one he used to live in with his mother, Wanda, prior to him going off to Newcastle for work. Brenda knew the layout, she'd been in there enough times for a shag or two many moons ago, and she'd be more relaxed now Wanda wasn't around. She'd died a couple of years back, the place standing empty ever since, and apparently, according to Cassie's contact at the hospital, who'd texted her not long ago, Vance had come back to snuff it. He had a heart condition, one that would need a donor dying to fix it, and he wasn't expected to last much longer.

That could be tricky. She may not have enough time to secure the cash withdrawal. Still, Vance was an only child and didn't have cousins or anything like that, his father and Wanda only children themselves.

No one to question him taking money out.

This sort of scenario was perfect.

Cassie's other contact, a woman who worked in a bank, stated Wanda had left eighty grand to Vance by putting it into his account just before she'd died—probably so he avoided inheritance tax—and he had seventy-five of it left. Who the fuck didn't have a big spend when handed that sort of cash?

She remembered then, how he'd always been frugal, his version of a gift for a girlfriend a glass of voddy down The Donny and a fat spring roll from the Jade on the way home, curry sauce to dip it in if you were lucky. No flowers, no jewellery, no little weekend holidays full of sauce between the sheets, the kind of thing she'd always wished for but had never got. That was why she'd binned him off—well, that and his well weird need to keep sucking her nipples even when they weren't having sex. Watching *Eastenders* with him doing that was strange as eff.

He didn't have the potential to keep her in any state of luxury, and Brenda had ambitions in that regard. She'd been young and in need of a good life where money wasn't scarce. She'd turned to Lenny not long after she'd dumped Vance, offering any services he thought she'd excel at, and this scam had been born.

God, those were the days, and she hadn't had an empty belly since, nor had her bank balance gone into the red. Of course, she got paid cash when it was a big chunk and had a 'wage' going into the Halifax which sorted her bills—Lenny had her down as an employee at the meat factory so the taxman didn't have to wonder owt.

She gathered her fake papers from the passenger seat and hung her carer's lanyard around her neck. Her reflection in the rearview mirror showed she'd been crying—and God had she cried at that bloody funeral—her eyes rimmed with red, the whites bloodshot. She'd loved Lenny—as a friend, nothing untoward going on, cheers very much—and would miss his laughter and the way he treated her like a sister. She'd have done anything for him but had, on occasion, got her own way without him realising it. She'd done what she'd told Jason to do, letting Lenny think her ideas were his.

And it was a lie, what she'd said. She wouldn't answer to Jason without a fuss if he made it to the top because she'd warn Cassie, who'd stop him getting there. Ensuring she had a secure wage was the most important thing, and Cassie would hopefully be pleased she'd foiled Jason's plan. Brenda never wanted to go down Poverty Road again if she could help it. Jason would learn it was survival of the fittest, and she was Olympian standard.

In relatively tarty gear, enough to get Vance's eyes popping, she left the car and trotted up his garden path, her newish heels pinching her toes.

He must be well old by now, wrinkly and all sorts, so she'd have to hide her shock upon seeing him, still get him to think she fancied him even when she wouldn't.

Bell button pushed, she slapped on a smile and hugged the papers to her chest. If any neighbours looked out, they'd think she was here to visit an old friend, nothing to worry about. This would be one of the easiest ones yet. So long as Vance didn't die mid-shag, she was golden.

She had all her patter ready and would filter it to him throughout the rest of the day and into the evening—if he let her stay. For all she knew, he could still have angsty feelings towards her for dumping him, slamming the door in her face. Okay, they'd seen each other since then, between her severing their sexual ties and him moving to Newcastle, but the times they'd bumped into each other had been strained.

No, he'd never forgiven her.

But she'd make up for it now. And she'd endure the nipple thing.

He opened the door, and while his features were the same, they sagged with age, wrinkles thick where they'd only been suspicions before, the salt-and-pepper strands of old now full-on sugar. She bit back a gasp and smiled.

"Vancey! How lovely to see you again." She waggled her lanyard which had her photo on it and some fake wordage, and at the top, the NHS logo. "I'm your carer. Who would have thought it, eh?"

"Carer?" He grunted. "I didn't ask for no carer."

"Well, that's the NHS for you, they don't always get in contact or make themselves clear. Maybe you got a letter sent but it went astray?" It was her usual bollocks, but even after saying it to so many old men, it didn't feel right. The NHS had been good to her mam when she'd been ill, and they'd offered Brenda counselling after she'd died. Funny how the thought of being poor again meant she'd say anything, do anything to earn money. "So, if you don't mind that it's me, shall we get started?"

He grunted again. "Fucking hell. Come away in."

He ambled off, his assured stride from years ago replaced by a pitiful shuffle, and she supposed if his ticker was on its way out, he got breathless if he moved too fast. It must take him ages to get anywhere. That might be a problem an' all. How would he get to the bank when the time came? She had to have cash, no bank transfers allowed. No sticky trails.

She scented food, the cloying stench of chip fat loitering in the air, and it reminded her of the grub she'd fed Michael that last day. Stuffing him and that debacle to the back of her mind, she followed Vance through to the living room, where he lowered himself into Wanda's flowery armchair, the one that was deemed only hers, no one else allowed to park their arse on it.

Vance caught his breath, his face sweaty, skin pasty.

Oh dear. This really didn't look good. It appeared he had less time than they'd been told. The text to Cassie had assured at least two months, but Vance seemed close to the Pearly Gates. They were opening up to admit him right this minute.

Brenda sat on the sofa, ankles together, knees spread so he could imagine what was between her legs at the top in the darkness of her short skirt. "I have papers here for you to sign, saying you're happy for me to come in each day and cook, clean, make you cups of tea, bathe you and whatever."

"Don't need no bathing. I've got Mam's shower with the seat in it."

"Of course you do." She launched into her spiel, sounding professional, someone who had proper credentials, all learnt on the job in the early days by speaking to a nurse friend, and later down the line on the internet. "So that's about it. Any questions?"

"Why did you leave me?"

Oh. They were going down that road, were they.

She could hardly tell him about the nipples so opted for a lie. "I wasn't the right woman for you, Vancey. You deserved better."

"You *were* the best."

"No, I wasn't. I walked away so you could find your soul mate." *Fucking hell, that sounded naff.* "I've never had anyone serious since, you know." *Liar.* "I realised I'd made a mistake but didn't have the bottle to come and tell you. Thought you'd toss me out on my ear."

He sighed. "I never would have done that. All those years wasted…"

She perked up for his benefit. "Could we try again now? Make up for lost time?"

He let out a nasty little laugh which sounded as if phlegm was trapped, trying to break free. "I've only got about two months left—if I'm lucky."

"Two months is still two months. There's a lot you can cram into that time, Vancey…"

Chapter Seventeen

*A*lisha Colson couldn't stand not knowing where Dave was. He still hadn't come home. Last night, she'd phoned his mobile and the garage but got no answer. Then she'd gone to the garage, finding the lights on and one of the double doors open a bit. He hadn't been in the pit, although a car was parked over *it on the ramps, and the lamp was on down there so he must have been working on it like he'd said.*

He hadn't lied.

So where was he?

She'd closed the door but didn't lock it in case he came back, then she'd gone home and phoned the police, but they'd told her to wait forty-eight hours. With no help from the coppers forthcoming, she'd contacted Karen Scholes, the grapevine of the estate — or the grassvine, whichever way you wanted to look at it — determined that someone would give a shit and help her. Karen promised to write about the disappearance in a late-night edition of The Life. *Someone might know where Dave had gone and come forward.*

Alisha hadn't made it to work today. She couldn't stand behind the counter in the little shop on her side of the Barrington and serve customers who'd want to speculate where her husband had vanished to. She knew what they'd be thinking, that he had a bit on the side and had run off with her, a new woman able to give him children. But Dave wasn't like that, he adored Alisha, he'd said so hundreds of times.

None of it made sense.

Confused, she idly washed up a mug from her morning cuppa, staring through the kitchen window at the back garden that needed a bit of a mow. The grass bent over, green arcs, the ground waterlogged from all that insane rain they'd had.

The garden would have to wait then. Dave reckoned if you used an electric mower on wet grass you'd get electrocuted. Alisha had done it before and she was still here, but there was no telling him.

Now she thought about it, he had been acting oddly recently, more anal than usual about her not going near his office in the spare bedroom. Jumpy he was, nervous. That had set her off wondering what he had

273

to hide, so when he was out, she'd tried turning the handle, all the while knowing it'd be locked, as usual.

She'd never found out where he kept the key, had never asked him why she couldn't go in there. Maybe she should have. Then she'd know if he was up to something, which he had to be. You didn't just walk out of your life, did you, unless you had no choice.

Was he hiding shit in there for Lenny or something? That wouldn't be a shock. He cleaned Lenny's cars after certain jobs—Alisha wasn't meant to know, but Dave told her everything. By the way Lenny looked at her sometimes, he knew she knew. It was all very awkward.

So if that were the case, Dave hiding stuff, what was with him being furtive, meeting up with some friend of his every night for weeks on end? A friend he refused to name, saying she wouldn't know who he was anyroad. Dave had said it was about work, maybe taking on an employee, but he'd never done that before, had always run the garage on his own. And as for going off at night… They usually spent the evenings he wasn't working watching telly side by side on the sofa. It had been strange to sit there alone.

What if he wasn't meeting a friend? What if it was a woman like the residents would assume? Oh God, she couldn't handle an affair. Couldn't stand seeing his new bird walking around with a fat belly, his child inside. Then them strolling through town pushing a buggy. Dave had told her if they didn't get lucky and have a child, he'd stick by her side. What if he'd changed his mind?

The doorbell pinged, and she wiped her wet hands on a tea towel, abandoning the washing up she hadn't even wanted to start in the first place. She trudged through to the hallway, not wanting to see anyone, to talk, but it could be a visitor with a sighting. She stared at the shape behind the patterned glass in the front door. It was tall and wide, the clothing dark. Maybe a copper? Did they have news?

Oh fuck. Had they found Dave dead in a ditch or something?

She rushed forward to open up, gasping at the sight of Lenny Grafton on her step. Had he been given information about Dave? It would be just like the big man to deliver it personally rather than go through Karen or Sharon if it was something shocking.

"I need to come in," he said.

Those were the words they all dreaded on the Barrington, coming from him. It meant, like it did with the police, that something dreadful had happened, news to be told indoors rather than where the neighbours could cop an earful, where they could stand behind their nets and watch your face crumple, then get straight on the phone to spread the word that something was going on: "Come quick, Alisha's having a meltdown. Something must have happened to The Mechanic."

She stepped back, an automatic action, unsteady, her legs going to jelly, and led the way to the kitchen. She left him to close up and dumped her hands back into the bubbles, continuing the washing up so she was occupied, had something to do other than imagine the worst. But what else could it be with Lenny here?

He came in and stood beside her, leaning his arse against the worktop. His grey suit looked expensive, as did his perfectly ironed white shirt. Two buttons were undone at the neck, and a sprout of chest hair poked up. "Dave's been sent to a lady called Marlene. She's someone who works for me now, helps me end things."

"Oh fuck, oh fucking hell," she whispered, grief hitting her instantly, sharp and biting and wicked and… "What…what the hell did he do?" Then all thoughts of him going missing, Dave hurt somewhere, *in pain, fled from her mind as if her previous worries had all been fabricated so she didn't have to face the truth until now. For Lenny to mention the ending of things, Dave must have done wrong, properly wrong, but what that could be she had no idea. He did things to help Lenny out, she knew that, but otherwise he was a good man.*

Wasn't he?

"He admitted some stuff." Lenny stared through to the hallway.

Shit, was he expecting someone else to arrive? Someone who'd help him 'chat' to her? Did he suspect her of wrongdoing, too? Everyone knew how devoted she was to Dave, so it stood to reason they'd imagine she'd know if he was up to bad things.

Lenny sniffed. "Now, I'm going to ask you a couple of questions, and if you lie to me, you'll be seeing Marlene an' all."

She stilled her hands in the water and looked at him. The idea of a woman killing people for him was somehow more sinister than a man, and a chill wended its way up her spine and fizzled out as goosebumps all over her head, drawing her scalp tight. "I have nowt to lie about. Nowt. So ask away."

"What's with Dave's office upstairs?"

Alisha frowned. What the hell did that have to do with Dave going missing? With…with this Marlene being the last person he ever saw as well as Lenny?

She took a deep breath. "He does his accounts up there for the garage. Got a desk and computer. The usual. What about it?"

Did Dave have information on that computer? Had he made a dossier on Lenny, stuff that could get the big man right in the shit? If he did, Alisha wanted nothing to do with it. Dave was insane if he'd plotted to take Lenny down.

"Can I go and have a look?" Lenny asked.

"If you want to kick the door down, be my guest. It's always locked. And I'd appreciate you fixing anything you break." She shouldn't have said that. If Lenny wanted to make a mess, he'd make a mess, and if he didn't want to put it right afterwards, he wouldn't. And if Dave had done something rotten, enough to be killed, Alisha had no right to demand anything. She told herself to shut up and give him standard answers, no elaborating.

"Been in there recently?" he asked.

"Like I said, always locked." She waved her hands in the water, and an unseen piece of food from last night's dinner plate wafted past her fingers. She shuddered.

"What were you doing Sunday?" he asked.

Eh? What sort of question was that? She didn't have to think long. "I went shopping. At the precinct. Bought some new shoes for work. Why?"

"Did you know Dave kept Jess Wilson in that office?"

She gaped at Lenny, her body freezing, her knees sagging. Her heart stopped for a few seconds, and she couldn't think, couldn't compute what he'd just said. Jess Wilson? Why would Dave have her in his office?

"What?" she managed. No, this couldn't be happening. She couldn't have heard him right.

"I've had a phone call. He was the one who took her, along with someone else, and when I asked him who that was, your husband told me to fuck off. Now, I wondered whether it was you in the back of that van, because to tell me to fuck off means he was protecting someone. Am I going to find brown leather gloves in this house?"

"What are you on about? I was at work when she was taken, ask my bloody boss. It'll be on CCTV."

What the fucking hell had Dave been thinking? Snatching a babby? Was it so they could keep her for their own because she couldn't have any? They'd have had to move away if that's what he had in mind. People would recognise the girl. Alisha would never have gone along with it, never. That child belonged to Joe and Lou, no one else.

"He's been meeting a friend lately," she said. "He wouldn't tell me his name. Most nights for weeks. Maybe he's the one in the back of the van. Maybe he's the one who phoned you."

Lenny pondered that for a moment. "You could be right. Where did he meet him?"

"He said the pub, so I assumed The Donny where he always goes."

"Why was he meeting him?"

She felt cornered, badgered. "He said it was for work."

Lenny dished out another verbal blow. "He took her for ransom, so he could pay for IVF."

Alisha's heart hurt. While what he'd done was terrible, he'd done it for her. But she couldn't forgive him for it, not when Jess had… "Did he kill her? Is that why he had to go and see this Marlene woman?"

"He said he didn't, said the kid wandered out of here by herself on Sunday while you were at the shops, but I didn't believe him, so I let Marlene have him. He's gone, no trace of him left behind, I saw to that myself. I don't want a child-killing bastard on my patch, won't stand for it, and he had to go. Now, you're going to get hold of Karen Scholes again and tell her this…"

She listened to what he had to say, the cover story, the news about a new woman on his books called Marlene, and throughout, Alisha washed the dishes and dried them after, put them away, all normal actions, ones that were at odds with his words. He made some tea while he talked, telling her he'd be looking for the person in the back of the van next, and when he found them, they were mincemeat.

"I left a message for you on the computer in the garage," he said, "one you'll tell Karen about. You'll go there and read it, then phone the police, tell them. There was a shotgun, boilersuit, and balaclava in the filing cabinet, so I got rid of those—we don't want the coppers asking any questions about them, and with Jess being taken at gunpoint, we definitely don't want them looking in Dave's direction, otherwise you'll have them on your doorstep, accusing."

Lenny was going to look after her. Thank God.

He handed her a cuppa. "Only limited people will know what he did to Jess, you got that?"

Alisha nodded. She didn't want the shame of it if Lenny announced it to everyone, of people looking at her funny and thinking she'd been the person in the back of the van. "I won't be saying owt."

"Make sure you don't, else you'll be tarred with his stinking brush. Word will spread quietly that the person has been dealt with, that we don't need to worry about that scummy kid-snatching fucker anymore. It'll all die down eventually, and Dave's remains will never be found. The person involved in that side of it owes me now and won't dare say owt about where he is. As far as anyone's concerned, Dave left you. Now then, drink your brew, and I'll nip you down to the garage so you can read that note. The sooner we get the word out the better."

Chapter Eighteen

The Barrington Life – Your Weekly

NEWS ON THE MECHANIC!

Karen Scholes – All Things Crime in our Time
Sharon Barnett – Chief Editor

TUESDAY EVENING. JULY 1ˢᵀ 1997

Just a quick note to let you know not to bother worrying about Dave Colson no more. Alisha came round this aft to tell me he's fucked off. No, she doesn't mind who knows it. In fact, she asked me to air her dirty laundry for her. She's raging, absolutely livid. He'd worked late Sunday and left her a note on the computer in the garage, one of them Dear John wotsits, except it said Dear Alisha. And he didn't even have the decency to write it by hand, he'd typed it on his computer. The upshot is, he can't hack being with someone who can't have kids and has pissed off with another bint.

Now, I don't know about you, but let's say if I ever see him again, there'll be trouble. Who does that? Who walks away from someone they love because their nethers don't work right? Fucking disgusting. I don't think he loved her at all really, but that's just my opinion.

Lenny wants a word with him, as you can imagine, so if anyone knows where The Mechanic has gone, let us know through the usual channels. He needs to apologise in person for what he's done to our Alisha, up and leaving like that. Wanker.

In other news, Lenny's asked me to pass on the fact he has a new employee. Her name's Marlene, and if you misbehave, she's the last person you'll see in your sorry little lives. Any coppers reading this, mind your own. The Barrington lives by its own set of rules, not yours, and you know it. Especially you, a certain someone who turns a blind eye here because he's too scared to do otherwise. You know who you are, Mr Plod. Keep on walking the beat, blinkers on, there's a good lad.

Chapter Nineteen

Dry-eyed and stiff upper lips in place, Cassie and Francis went to the meat factory. Cassie had sent Jason off to do the rounds with the those who looked after any needs of the residents in the high-rise—plumbers, electricians, the cleaners who mopped the main foyer floors and kept the lifts from smelling of piss. He hadn't been pleased, said he should be by her side all the time, not her mam, but Francis wanted to see some old friends, so it was a social visit as well.

Mam had worked at the factory when Dad first bought it, right there in the thick of it, basically running the place beside Joe while her husband concentrated on building up the Barrington business. Maybe Mam was feeling nostalgic at the minute, but she'd woken this morning saying she wanted to go 'back to work', and Cassie had indulged her.

While Mam caught up with Sheryl and Pauline, her old pals from years back—they hadn't had a chance to natter at the wake—Cassie toured the factory as a normal owner would.

She sought out William Dougherty in his office—he managed the place but had no idea what went on after dark some nights. Dad had

292

said he was on the verge of asking him the very question Cassie was about to, but then he'd got under the weather and died, so he hadn't had the chance.

Cassie sat in the chair opposite William's desk. "I've got an extra job for you of a morning, first thing before anyone else comes in, but only on specific mornings. I'll text you the night before."

William nodded, eager to please, elbows propped on his chair arms, hands steepled beneath his chin. One middle finger poked into the divot he had there. "What's that then?" His eyes lit up—from the new responsibility he suspected she was about to offer, or did he think he'd get a raise because of the extra work?

"You've heard of a Marlene, I take it." She gave him one of her glares.

"Yes… Everyone knows about Marlene."

"Dad was going to bring you in on her, who she is, what needs doing with her."

"Right..." William appeared uncomfortable, shifting from side to side.

"Don't crap your kecks. She's the old mincer, a modified one with a chute in the side room."

"Oh." He shuffled about, clearly unnerved. "So it's not...not a woman?"

"No. She chews up bodies."

"Shit."

"I trust you can keep that to yourself." She paused, wondering if Dad had made the right call with him. "After all, if you don't, you'll find yourself inside her."

"Of course. I'm not likely to tell anyone." He blinked, looking everywhere but at her.

Why couldn't he meet her eye? Had he just *lied* to her?

"Make sure you don't," she said. "Now then, the people who use the mincer are getting on a bit, no need for you to know who they are, and I want you to check it each morning after it's used to ensure she's properly clean. Who knows if they'll miss a bit of flesh. While the old mincer isn't in use as such, there are still standards to uphold, what with inspections because Marlene is on the property. I can't be doing with Health and Safety issuing any warnings."

The meat factory had to be a legitimate front, clear of any wrongdoing.

William held both hands up, palms facing her, as if he unconsciously pushed her away, out of his face, his life. "No problems from me, I assure you."

"Good. If I find out different, you know what the score is." She stood. "You have a wife, yes?"

His face paled. "Please…"

Curious, she asked, "What did you think I meant by that?"

"You'll hurt her if I say owt."

"Um, no. Never assume when it comes to me. What I mean is, it would be a shame to put her through a missing person kind of scenario, wouldn't it. Imagine her worry, how upset she'd be that you've vanished."

He swallowed, and it seemed his throat was tight. "Look, I know what goes on, what you are. I know what your dad was. I'm still here."

Oh, you have no idea what I am, a woman ruled by her monster.

"Fine." She left the office, his phrasing telling her more than he probably realised. 'What' you are. 'What' your dad was. Not 'who'. He saw them as things, not people. Maybe as despicable creatures. *All the more reason to do as he's told then.*

296

But it hurt, what he'd said, and she didn't understand why. What did she care how he thought of her?

It was the way he looked at me. Like I'm a piece of shit.

She barged back into the office, startling him, the cup of coffee in his hand going flying, liquid spilling on the desk, the cup falling to the floor.

"For your information, if you ever imply I'm 'less than' again, I'll do for you, understand?"

She stormed away, cursing herself for making a mistake, a judgement error in asking him to check Marlene. Yes, he'd do as she'd told him and keep quiet about it, but if anyone put him under pressure, he'd crack, tell all, she was sure of it.

What had Dad been thinking? Or wasn't he on his game near the end?

She thought about his trips into the past, wanting to tell her stories.

Had he been more bothered about what was *than what* is?

To calm her flurrying thoughts, she strutted through the long fridge room, inspecting the carcases hanging there, for quality and to check they'd been sold the best beef, lamb, and pork. The pork she could guarantee—Joe provided it— and once again she thought of people eating human meat in with their piggy goods. Okay, it had been digested by the animals, but traces of it must still be there.

Someone, somewhere, would have Richie Prince in their breakfast sausages by now.

Dad had found that side of things funny. Cassie didn't, but where else could they dispose of the human mince? The idea of getting caught like Dennis Nilsen by lobbing it all down the toilet didn't appeal.

No, they had the perfect scheme going, and it would be foolish to change it now. It had worked for twenty-three years, started when Dad had killed The Mechanic. And that reminded her to nip and see Joe and Lou. Their debt had been paid in full now Dad was dead, so as the agreement stood, if they didn't want their pigs fed anymore, Cassie would *have* to find an alternative.

She left the fridge and met up with Felix, who oversaw the packaging—mince, of all things. She led him into an office and closed the door. "How are you today?"

Felix sat, his knees cracking. "Fine and dandy, considering. I'm still a bit heartsore over your dad, but shit happens and we move on, don't we."

"We do. Look, I need you to have a chat with William Dougherty." She explained what had occurred.

"So he needs to understand the way of things a bit more."

"Yes."

Felix nodded. "He'll know by the time you leave here."

She gifted him one of her genuine smiles. "Thank you. And there's a job coming your way later. Tonight."

"Ah. Someone chancing their arm?"

Cassie nodded. "Yes. Despite me giving warnings that everything should stay the same, Nathan Abbott thought it was a good idea not to play by the rules. I knew it would happen with someone, so it's no surprise. Jason's issued him with a couple of verbals since Dad died, but Nathan's taken it upon himself to skim off some of the sex worker earnings, like we wouldn't notice, so I'll be going to see him about eight. Show him who's boss. Got myself a new weapon, too."

"A fucking little weasel, he is. Lenny only took him on as a favour to Nathan's dad. Your father and Nathan's were mates at school, see. Nathan had been on the way to ruin, the demon drink, and his dad wanted him to have a focus."

"Hmm."

"So what's this weapon then?" Felix raised his bushy grey eyebrows.

"Just something I thought up. I made it yesterday."

"*Made* it?"

Cassie smiled again. "He'll be in a bit of a state when you pull the tarpaulin back, so be aware of blood transfer."

"Fuck me, kid, what are you up to?"

"You'll find out in *The Life*."

"I see. Like that, is it?"

"People need to understand I won't rely on guns and knives, quick deaths, minimal pain. If they think they're going to get tortured, it'll keep them in line better."

"Lenny wouldn't—"

"No, he wouldn't, but *I* would."

Felix nodded, thoughtful. "I see. Bloodthirsty, are you?"

"No, just making a point. I'm a woman. People think they can take the piss. I'm going to show them they can't."

Plus I want to see how far I can push myself, how evil my monster is. Nathan will be my guinea pig.

Felix worried about Cassie. All this talk of homemade weapons and meting out a different kind of justice to Lenny had his skin crawling. All right, Felix and his cousin minced people, but that was acceptable behaviour in order to dispose of the bodies. The code had always been to shoot or stab, give people a good kicking beforehand if necessary, and sometimes Lenny strangled folks until just before they died, but Felix had a feeling what Cassie had in mind went down the callous route.

Times changed, he knew that, and people did an' all, evolving into something 'other'. Himself and Ted had changed, too, moving here to start at the factory, and never in a million years would they have thought they'd be a party to murder. The stubby penknives of the old days had been

303

replaced with long-bladed swords and machetes over the years, but *that* kind of progression was understandable. To make something yourself in this day and age could only mean a new level of pain for the recipient.

He'd get an idea once he saw the body, and if he thought Cassie had gone too far, he'd have a quiet word with Francis. Surely she wouldn't condone this sort of thing. Life was supposed to stay the same after Lenny's death, no go down a different motorway.

Still, it wasn't like he could complain to Cassie, was it. Whether he'd given her sweets or not if she'd passed their stall on the market every Saturday, or handed over a few coins as pocket money, she'd treat him like everyone else, warning him to keep his opinions to himself.

Or she'd use her new tool on him.

He sighed and left the office, off to find Ted, who worked in another packing area. He was on the lamb chop section, so Felix ambled over there, pulling his cousin aside to give him his thoughts.

"She *made* a weapon?" Ted whispered.

"Yeah. She had a right mad glint in her eye an' all when she told me about it. Seems she's gone off the rails a bit with her old man dying."

"Or she's coming into her own." Ted eyed the ceiling. "It might be what's needed. You've heard the whispers before Lenny snuffed it and Cassie took over some of the running. They don't like it that she's female. She's got a point to prove, that's all. She'll make it with this newfangled thing of hers then that'll be it, back to guns and blades."

"I hope so." Felix shivered, and not from the chilled air. "I wouldn't want to see her getting herself into hot water."

Chapter Twenty

Night had fallen, the deepest, darkest kind prevalent in the countryside, thicker somehow, menacing, disguising more than in cities and towns. This was as close to the countryside as they were going to get. On the outskirts, near where New and Old Barrington met, a mile or so away from the squat, Cassie sat in the passenger seat, Jason beside her behind the wheel. He'd parked beneath a tree with low-hanging branches, the willow's frost-speckled swishing branch skirt partially hiding them from view. Had this been in summer, they wouldn't be able to see ahead for the leaves.

Headlights off, they sat waiting for Nathan Abbott to walk through the pitch-black clearing ahead. He came this way nightly from his dingy one-bed on Old Barrington to ensure his charges had come to work, his destination the edge of the woods beside the main road out of town. This location kept the sex workers off the residential streets and away from the bobbies, and tree trunks made for excellent propping posts where the women rested their backs while punters got their jollies. Fumbles al fresco or in the backs of cars.

The five under Nathan's watch had been forewarned an hour ago and had caught the bus round to The Donny, their wages paid to keep them out of the way for the rest of the night. Keep their mouths shut. It was worth the cash payout to catch Nathan, no witnesses. The ladies had been told he needed a kicking, he'd been palming their hard-earned money, so of course, they'd been only too happy for him to get his due. They weren't to breathe a word of it, though. If she found out they had, they knew what would happen.

No one had argued.

Cassie would appoint a new handler—she didn't like the word 'pimp'. Maybe Trevor could manage them, or Lisa would be a better bet.

No, they gossiped. God, there was so much to remember. *A new man then, or maybe one of the other handlers who run the women in town.*

"What's this weapon of yours then?" Jason asked, his query breaking the silence.

Cassie was enjoying the subterfuge, having something only she and Mam knew about for now. She adjusted her night-vision goggles— they were a bit tight beneath her eyes. "You'll find out when I use it, won't you."

She'd practised on the skin-and-fat side of a slab of beef taken from the factory, which she'd hung in their shed with Mam's help, mainly to see the effect of it on the skin, what kind of mess she could expect if she factored in the amount of blood that would leak. Nathan would look a fucking wreck, but it was no more than he deserved. The question was, she had to hope her monster took over, because otherwise, she wouldn't be able to go through with it.

"You don't steal from a Grafton, and especially not after warnings," Mam had said earlier. "This weapon, it'll show them all, and Nathan will realise he picked the wrong women to fleece."

Sometimes, since Dad's death, Mam acted more eager to hurt people than Cassie. It was strange to see her mother's eyes sparkling with the excitement of what Cassie had to do. Cassie had never seen his side of her before, and it would take a bit of getting used to. Mind you, if Mam got a thrill out of it, Cassie didn't have to feel so bad that she did, too. She wasn't alone, someone else understood. What she struggled with was, if she and Mam were basically good people, how could they run the Barrington with its drugs and sex workers, Marlene, and the pigs?

Good people wouldn't even contemplate having anything to do with that.

Jason toyed with the coil of thin blue rope on his lap, something Cassie had told him to bring. "Do you think he'll run when he cops sight of us?"

"Probably, but that's what your gun's for. Imagine he's a rabbit scarpering over a field. Shoot him in the leg to bring him down." She'd recited something Dad had once said. A sigh came out of her, and she turned to check out Jason's goggles. "He'll shit himself seeing you coming at him with those on, let alone me."

Jason laughed. "Little bastard." He concentrated through the windscreen. It had fogged up a tad, so he cranked the side window down an inch or two. "This is what we're made for, you and me. Hurting people together, bringing them in line. I told you I'll protect you, do anything you want, and I meant it."

Cassie had to admit he'd been all right lately. Annoying but all right. "Hmm."

He reached over and rested a hand on her thigh. "Have you thought any more about…you know?"

She took his hand away and dropped it on his leg, patting it as if to say: *That's* where it belongs, not on me. That was a movement too far on his part. She hadn't given permission for him to touch her intimately. "Let me get my feet properly under the table first. I've got to put everything I have into the business at the minute. I can't think about seeing you when I have so much to brush up on. My head's full of work. There's no room for more." That excuse should hold him off.

"No reason why we can't go out for a meal or whatever when we discuss the business, is—"

"Shh. What's that?" Her heart pounded. Movement to the far right, by a tree. The crackle of a footstep coming in through the open window.

"It's him." Jason sucked in a deep breath and hung the rope around his neck. "Come on."

Cassie squinted, made Nathan out. He stepped past a tree into the clearing, his clothing a weird green hue through her goggles. His coat hood covered his narrow head and, hands in his pockets, he strode with purpose.

"Right, it's a go," she said.

They shot out of the car, and Cassie ran for their target, her boots thudding on the hard crispy ground. Adrenaline pushed her on—she was doing this, acting out one of the stories Dad had told her growing up, collaring some bastard in the woods—and she imagined what Nathan saw in the darkness, her and Jason in black clothing, the weird goggles, them streaking towards him, eerie moving shadows over the spiky, white-rimed grass.

Nathan stopped and stared for a moment, lowering his hood. "What the...?"

Then he bolted towards the other side of the clearing, aiming for the trees where he'd come out near the place the women usually stood. Safety in numbers, was that his reckoning? Hiding behind a line of sex workers, letting them do the bartering for him? Cassie laughed, loving the thrill of the chase, and gave the order.

"Get the rabbit."

Jason fired, his silencer on, and Nathan went down howling. He'd been caught in the right calf and rolled around on the grass, his knee pulled up to his chest. He hugged it, wailing, and Cassie slowed, coming to a stop near him by the left-hand tree line. Why hadn't he gone back the way he'd come, which was closer to civilisation? Or did he actually care about the women and had planned to protect them? If so, why draw a gunman and his accomplice *towards* them?

He couldn't be thinking straight.

Jason switched on the torch attached to the top of his night-vision goggles and pointed the beam Nathan's way.

Their quarry stared up at her, his eyes wide, his skin so pale in the splash of light. Tears stained his cheeks, his lips blanched and stretched into a one-sided grimace.

"What...what the fuck's...all this in aid of?" he panted out.

"Don't play innocent, you utter piss-taker." Cassie kicked his bad leg.

Nathan screamed.

"Fuck me, a bit of a noisy bastard, aren't you?" she shouted above the din. "Anyone would think you'd been shot." She laughed again, enjoying this a bit too much.

"Oh God, it's you…"

"Yeah, it's me. You know what this is about. You've had a visit from me after Lenny died; I told you the score. You've had visits from Jason despite that. Now I'm involved."

"What the *hell* are you on about?" Nathan asked.

"So you're going to lie, are you?" Cassie switched her head torch on so the brightness splashed into his eyes. "You're going to make out my right hand hasn't come to warn you before now?"

Nathan rapid-blinked. "Too right. I haven't seen Jason other...other than to pass the takings over. Aww, fuck, that hurts. He's not said...owt to me about no...warning. Jesus Christ..."

"That's the issue," she said. "The takings. They're down."

Nathan tried to get up but abandoned it to lie flat, legs and arms in a star shape. Dark splodges marred his trouser leg, also at his groin where he'd pissed himself. "Those takings are on...the up, the women have been...making more lately. Them being down is bullshit."

"What you gave me doesn't work out right, pal," Jason said.

"I *told* you they were up."

"Did you fuck." Jason shook his head, the torchlight shooting side to side and picking out slim trunks and the blackness in between. "I got in my car after picking them up from you and counted it, and three times they were down. You're skimming."

Nathan pushed himself up to sitting. "No. *No.* The past three payments have all been...over a hundred more than usual—for each woman, so that's like a...grand more every time I've handed it over."

Cassie butted in. "They were a hundred *down,* so if you're saying they were up, that means you were taking eleven hundred off the top of the totals, you thieving little wanker. What's that then, three thousand three hundred since you started this scheme?"

Nathan gritted his teeth. Shut his eyes. Tears squeezed out, probably from the pain of the gunshot wound. "*He's* skimming then. Do you think I'm stupid enough to do it when *this* is the sort of shite that happens? I *know* how it is on the Barrington. I grew up knowing it."

"You would say that." Jason pressed his boot sole on Nathan's wounded leg, covering the exit wound.

The man cried out, face scrunching in pain. He breathed through his teeth, the air hissing in and out, cheeks shuddering. Sweat coated his even paler face, and he whimpered. "I…didn't…skim. I was upfront and honest and—"

"Get the rabbit," Cassie said.

Jason shot Nathan's shin on his other leg. While the dickhead flailed around, Cassie had no desire to watch him suffer so jogged to the car to get her weapon. She opened the boot, then her briefcase, and stared at the shiny wooden handle inside, the thick leather strand of the whip hidden by barbed wire coiled tight around it. A couple of spikes still had beef fat on them where the dishwasher hadn't cleaned it properly.

It didn't matter. Human flesh would be joining it soon.

She gripped the handle in her gloved hand and ran through the willow's hanging branches. They grasped at her hair as if to stop her. She legged it towards Nathan and Jason. In her absence, Jason must have forced their prey to stand, which would be agony, considering both legs had been shot. Who knew, bone may have been shattered.

Like she could allow herself to give a shit.

Cassie stopped in front of Nathan. "Take your clothes off."

"W...what?" He whined, an awful noise that slashed the still air. "Please...I didn't *do* anything."

She didn't believe him. Had never liked him *or* his deadbeat father. "Shut up. Now strip."

He struggled, of course he did, but Cassie stood by and watched, offering no assistance, her impatience growing thin at how long he was taking. Jason waggled the gun at him to speed things along and, an excruciating couple of minutes later, Nathan was naked, hugging himself and crying like the robbing wretch he was.

"Get into the woods," Jason ordered.

On the other side of this tree line was the road the women plied their trade on. Too far in and motorists would see them, so they'd previously agreed to get the job done a metre or two in from this side.

Nathan hobble-hopped, crying, sobbing every time a foot met with the ground. Foliage crunched, and a night bird cawed. A gust of wind blew the remaining leaves from autumn around them, whispering about torture and death and living by Lenny's rules: *Fool is the man who breaks them… What Lenny says goes…*

"Stop," Cassie said. "Put your back to that tree." She pointed so he'd be under no illusion as to which one she referred to.

Nathan obeyed, sniffling, snot dripping, and she asked herself why he didn't run, or try to, for the road. Perhaps he knew it was useless, what with Jason holding the gun, but Cassie, in the same situation, thought she might at least give it a go, especially with that rumble of a car engine breaking through the leaves' chatter. Even if he got shot again, he might make it, flag a motorist down, ask for help.

Jason used the rope to tie Nathan to the trunk, walking around and around until his neck was concealed, the rest of him the perfect palette for Cassie's barbed paintbrush. She ignored Nathan's blubbering, his denials, annoyed he tried to foist the blame on Jason, who'd *never* steal takings, she was sure of that much. He might be a prat sometimes, bossy and nosy, but he'd never do *that*. Maybe Nathan had scrabbled for some excuse, anything so he didn't get a third shot.

Anything so he didn't get what was coming to him.

Cassie stood about three feet away and parted her legs for a steadier stance. Jason aimed his head torch at Nathan, lighting him up further, a pitiful display, blood that appeared black dripping down his shins from the entry and exit wounds. Somewhere, the bullet casings waited for someone to find them, although if no one was looking for them specifically, they'd hopefully remain undetected. If they didn't, they'd be put down to poachers, because as well as Nathan the Big Quivering Rabbit here, there were others of the fluffy variety.

People hunted them illegally all the time.

She held her homemade weapon up. "Look at this, Nathan. Isn't it pretty?"

He let out a choked sob and shut his eyes.

"Fuck me," Jason whispered, but he was smiling, the gleam of bloodlust in his eyes. "That's grand, that is."

"I think so." Cassie smiled back.

And she swung that whip at Nathan's torso, the spikes sticking into him, same as they had with the beef, gripping his skin, spearing through to the layer of fat then the flesh beneath. Nathan's scream, she'd never heard anything like it, fear-laden, panic-laden, fuck-it's-the-end-of-my-life-laden.

She wrenched the barbs out and whipped him countless more times so his chest and belly were covered in mess. She admired it like Dad would have while Nathan keened, then moved to the side, launching another attack, across his face this time. The end of the whip coiled around the tree and attached to the bark. His lips punctured, and blood dripped from the holes in his cheeks, heading south to join the oozing liquid on his torso. Paint drips, that was what they looked like, those streams of red that were inky through the night-vision goggles, the torchlight picking them out as the stars of the show.

Jason walked around the tree to tug the spikes from the bark. "The state of him."

"One more go should do it," Cassie shouted over the noise coming from Nathan.

She held the handle out and, with a hefty side swipe, let the whip find its mark. The barbed tips munched into his cock, the tops of his thighs, and Nathan's new scream cut off, an abrupt dying of sound, his head slumping forward.

"Get him down." She walked to the car and placed her new best friend in the boot inside the plastic-lined briefcase, lifting the goggles so she could admire the blood and flesh in the sparkle of the interior light. It had worked well, given that scrote a ton of pain, and she'd use it again and again if she had to, until everyone got the message.

William Dougherty might be next.

She took a folded body bag from the back and strode to Jason. Nathan was out of it on the grass, and she dropped the bag then held her hand out.

"Give me the gun."

Jason passed it over, pouting if she was any judge, but she ignored his silly need to end

Nathan. This was Cassie's first kill as the boss, and she wasn't about to let her right hand have the pleasure. She aimed at Nathan's forehead, pulled the trigger, and stared, fascinated, his top half lifting, brain and blood spattering, and he flumped back down again. She studied the hole she'd made. The bullet would be deep in the ground, the blood and gore licked up by an urban fox later if fate was on their side. Or those little jumping rabbits if they turned carnivore.

She made a mental note to collect the rope and Nathan's clothes, his boots.

"Let's get him in the bag," she said. "Take him to the meat factory. I'd say that was a job well done, wouldn't you?"

The monster inside her roared.

Chapter Twenty-One

The Barrington Life – Your Weekly

NEW WEAPON IN CONTROLLING DEVIANTS

Karen Scholes – All Things Crime in our Time
Sharon Barnett – Chief Editor

For anyone wishing to challenge Cassie Grafton's authority, let's just say Cassie herself isn't averse to being the final face you'll see if you cross her. She's her father's daughter, yes, but make no mistake, she has a new weapon in her arsenal before you get to see the elusive Marlene or the Grim Reaper. A whip with barbed wire down the length. Think on that before you step out of line.

Karen saved the document and pushed up from her desk, leaving the computer to fall asleep. She'd print the note in the morning. She was too tired to do it tonight, then traipse the cold streets with Sharon and the helpers, not seeing her bed this side of midnight. Cassie had said that was okay, but to be honest, Karen would have argued against it if she'd insisted it be distributed now.

Cassie needed to know Karen wouldn't be bossed.

There was something about her Karen didn't like nowadays. It might be that she wasn't Lenny, a man she'd learnt to play over the years, to tolerate, and she was too old to be learning a new person all over again, their ways, their patterns, their thought process. Mind you, if she wanted to keep her five hundred a week, she'd have to.

Five hundred. She wanted more than that for this lark, especially now Cassie had informed her, not half an hour ago, that Doreen fucking Prince was coming in on *The Barrington Life*, giving her insight on matters. The pamphlet was Karen and Sharon's baby, had started out as a way to get the community spirit going on the estate just before Lenny had taken control, and also to pass on news that any hassle would be dealt with by them and a couple of blokes who didn't mind using their fists. But Lenny had come to demand they use it to pass on *his* news, too, and while she'd agreed because of the cash payment, plus he'd bought her a new computer, she'd felt a bit protective over their mini newspaper. Over their ruling of the patch, such as it was.

And now Cassie had stuck her oar in.

What the hell could Doreen contribute? Tips on knitting? How to bake the perfect loaf? Which horse to bet on?

Fucking hell…

Karen and Sharon were the pulse of information on the Barrington, and by rights, it should belong to them. She'd conceded defeat when Lenny had taken over, asking her bully boys to stand down—Lenny was a bloke and easily ousted them from what Karen considered was their reign over the estate, albeit at a much less abusive level than his—but with Cassie in charge, well, Karen quite liked the idea of taking the area back, at least the 'warning residents in person' side of things. Karen was in the know on who to use for threatening folks, and Jason Shepherd was at the top of her list, despite him being up Cassie's arse at the minute.

Years ago, Karen and Sharon had been the ones to go round and smooth out any argy-bargy. They'd listened to gossip and marched to houses, offering either support or a caution. Okay, they weren't as menacing as Lenny, but they did have a good right hook on them, and most people shied away through fear. With Lenny behind them, no one had dared mess with them, upping their status so that these days they were as feared as Lenny himself to a certain degree.

Karen like to think so anyroad.

Thugs, people called them, bullies, but that wasn't always true. If someone needed help, they were the first on the scene with a cuppa and a Tesco Victoria sponge, ready to put any grievances to rights.

She rang Sharon and explained matters. "So with Doreen here—Cassie said she had to come to my house to discuss what was going into *The Life*, for fuck's sake—we're not going to be able to put our subtle hints into the flyers without Doreen letting Cassie know what we're up to before we get a chance to post them."

"We'll send out a second one each week." Sharon coughed, hacking up a lung.

"Fuck me, love, stop smoking those ruddy fags."

"Knob off. Look, we'll need to have another think. We were pissed up when you thought about taking the estate back—things have changed, we're too old now to be gallivanting about like we used to, and I haven't lumped anyone for years. Besides, Cassie's a nutter, worse than Lenny so we've heard, so we need to reconsider."

"No, I want more control. If shit happens, *we're* to go back out there and deal with it, not get hold of *her* so she gets all the glory. She's got funny eyes, and people with funny eyes aren't right in the head in my opinion."

"Funny eyes? Listen, sleep on it. And send me the latest article so I can proof it while you're on the line."

"Hang on." Karen went back to her computer, wiggled the mouse to wake up the screen, and attached the Word document to an email. "Coming your way now."

"Shit, let me read it on the laptop cos I'm on the phone."

"You can still read an email on it while you're connected to me, you know."

"Bollocks to that, I'll end up cutting you off by mistake."

Karen waited. Listened to the noises—the clicking of a lighter, Sharon moving, sighing. A different kind of click, dulled, the tap of a mousepad.

"Oh, bloody Nora," Sharon screeched. "What the hell's she on with this weapon?"

"See what I mean now? Why we need to become top dogs again? You can't go round hitting people with something like that. I don't want her barbing residents. Before Lenny, we used our fists and feet, and our men had blades, then Lenny had knives and guns. *This* sort of shit? A step too far."

"I know, but if she finds out what we're up to, do you want to risk having barbed wire across *your* face?"

Karen didn't like the sound of that, not at her advanced age, but she was convinced she could topple Cassie without violence if given the chance.

You didn't know unless you tried, did you.

Chapter Twenty-Two

F elix pulled the tarpaulin back. Ted shone his torch on the body, the beam picking out swirls of dancing snow falling on the red wounds. They melted on contact.

"Oh, the great Lord above, what the fuck has she gone and done," Felix muttered, his heart sore for the sweet girl they'd once known. She'd gone down the darker path, that much was obvious. "What has Lenny created?"

"A woman who tortures. She's a new breed."

"She's something."

Felix didn't like the look of what the weapon had done. While she'd ended Nathan's life with a bullet to the head, putting the poor sod out of his misery, he'd been shot in the legs, too—overkill if you asked him. It was clear, going by the blood, that the new weapon had been used while he was still alive. Blood didn't run from the dead, not *this* dead anyroad. Holes decorated the skin, that skin torn where whatever had entered was snatched out. It seemed to have been removed with some force, a ripping effect, and the pain must have been immense. Some skin hung loose, triangles and strips of it, juicy flesh on the underside.

What had Cassie become? Yes, she'd grown hard once Lenny had brought her into the business properly, as if she adopted that persona for something to hide behind, but he'd never have put her down as someone who'd be mean for the sake of it.

This smacked of that. Of proving a point. Of her testing her own boundaries, the ones within, the ones that stopped you going too far.

"Could be her grief talking," Felix mused, wanting to justify her actions, to have a solid reason why she'd gone off the rails. "Like, she'll have a patch of doing shit like this then calm down. Maybe she can't grieve properly, doesn't know how to. Remember how Lenny was. You moved on immediately in his eyes, didn't let anything get you down, the business was the be all and end all. He passed that advice on to her.

I'm willing to bet he lectured her when he knew his heart was going to give out. Told her to boss the lot of us in a new way."

"I noticed Francis was hardened at the funeral and wake an' all," Ted said. "Not like her usual self at all."

"What's Lenny taught them? I mean, what's he *really* taught them?"

"To survive without him." Ted shook his head. "I reckon William Dougherty ought to count himself lucky that he won't end up like this."

"Hmm." Felix had told Ted what had happened, how he'd smoothed things over with the factory manager, although privately, he had his own ideas about Cassie opening her mouth to the man. "For what it's worth, it was a bad call on Lenny's part to bring William into the inner circle. Cassie was only doing what her father said, but you've got to be a certain person to be in the full know. You've got to be able to sleep at night despite the horrors. See it as a job, forget it when you go home. I'm as sure as I can be that William got the message, but saying that, there was something in his eyes I didn't like."

Ted scratched his nose. "As in…?"

"He'll do as he's told but won't hesitate to blart it all out if, say, a copper comes calling." And, just like that, the truth of it settled in Felix's bones. His gut was rarely wrong.

"Shit. Maybe he *will* end up like this then." Ted scrubbed at his chin, the stubble shushing.

Felix couldn't shake the feeling of dread. "I think he ought to go. Now. Before it gets to a sticky stage."

"Cassie won't like being told what to do."

Felix sighed. "Who said she'll be told? I'll word it in a way so she doesn't feel like I'm ordering

343

her around. Come on, let's get this fucker minced. It's cold, and it looks like the snow has a mind to settle. I prefer my bollocks defrosted, thanks."

Chapter Twenty-Three

At the noise of an engine grumbling, too close for it to be on the main road, Joe got up from the table and stared out into the night from his kitchen window. The fireplace crackled, blasting out comforting heat. It sounded like the flames were arguing, snapping at one another from some heated slight. A log popped, and he jumped a touch. He preferred coal, but Lou's brother had dropped round a load of wood. Joe could agree with his wife there—it did smell good.

The pigs were due a human feed soon, but not *this* soon. Headlights stabbed into the darkness, coming closer to the farmhouse. Surely Felix and Ted hadn't finished already.

"They're early," Lou said from the table behind him.

He smiled at her reflection, how she cradled a cup of tea, the pot close by beneath the stripy knitted cosy with its yellow bobble on top. "I thought the same thing."

Lou abandoned her tea and got up. She stood beside him, leaning into him, her cheek on his shoulder. "Don't forget to leave the barn doors open so I can watch."

She said the same every time.

He glanced down at her hands. She fiddled with the binoculars hanging around her neck. A bit macabre that, viewing things through those, but it was what his wife wanted, so he'd leave her be, like always. If she needed a close-up of the proceedings in order to sleep at night, to settle her grief that wouldn't leave her in peace, who was he to deny her need?

"Maybe you ought to come out there. Watch in the barn." A rum suggestion, but perhaps, if she was right in the thick of it, the horror may well stop her fascination with observing. It couldn't be healthy for her, seeing that. Couldn't be doing her well-being any good.

"Maybe."

Joe left the kitchen and, in the mudroom, stuck his feet into his chilly wellies, the cold seeping through his socks. As usual, the sight of Jess's little pink boots poked at his heart, but he hardened it and shrugged into his thick padded coat then pulled a hat on, tugging it down to cover his earlobes. The weather had taken a turn with the white flurries, and he hoped it didn't settle.

Weary—it had been a busy day—he opened the door, stepping out into the cold and snowy night, blinking at the headlights still on, pointing directly at him. Why hadn't the cousins parked their van by the barn? Maybe they'd thought to collect him and drive over, save his nose getting nipped by the wicked breeze.

They were a decent pair, Felix and Ted, despite what they did.

A shadow got out of the vehicle and walked into a tunnel of light, black clothing, hair swooshing to one side in the wind, a rippling red river, snow twisting around her.

What was *Cassie* doing here?

"Ted and Felix will be about an hour," she said. "But I've come to talk business. Sorry I haven't got round to it before tonight. Your debt's paid, as you're aware, but I want to offer you a deal. A grand every time the pigs are fed from now on."

"No." Lou came out to stand next to Joe, a tartan throw blanket around her. She hugged herself but stood tall. Taller than she had in a long while. "We'll do it for free. We will *always* owe for what Lenny did. His death doesn't change things."

Cassie frowned and gathered her wayward hair, tucking it to one side in the front of her coat. "Free?"

"I need it," Lou said. "I need to see it happen."

"I don't understand." Cassie stuffed her hands in her pockets and frowned.

"You don't need to," Joe said.

Chapter Twenty-Four

Nathan Abbott rested on the floor in the side room next to Marlene. Felix wondered where his clothes were and hoped Cassie remembered to burn them in the furnace at the squat like Lenny would have. It was one thing for her to play at being top dog while Lenny had been ill, but another entirely to have full responsibility without her father to fall back on. There were many things to remember and keep track of, but maybe Francis was there in the shadows, offering advice.

That woman knew the business as well as Lenny, although Felix doubted she knew everything her late husband had got up to. The strangling, for instance. His creepy need to throttle someone to the point of death then let them breathe again.

Felix had always thought that was fucking odd.

Maybe it explained Cassie and her new weapon. She probably had the nutter gene, same as Lenny, the need to go a little bit too far, just because she could.

"I'll phone Cassie about William now," Felix said to Ted. "Give her a chance to get over here while we mince this twat. Like Lenny taught us, don't put off what can be done now."

"All right." Ted squatted to inspect Nathan, his hands draped between his open knees. "This mess here is a tad ridiculous if you want to know the truth. We'll need to mop up. There's congealed blood on the floor. She's done what she's done without a thought to us two mugs." He sighed. "Ever think you're getting too old for this?"

"Sometimes." Felix took his phone out and connected the call. "But it's what we do. It pays the bills. Now *shh*."

Cassie answered on the first ring. "Who's in trouble?"

Felix thought about her new life-and-death rule regarding phone calls and winced at his error. "Sorry, I should have texted 'problem'. I'm used to ringing Lenny. Bear with me while I get used to the new way of things."

"What's the matter?" She sounded impatient, annoyed with him.

She probably saw him as some old doddering duffer and didn't reckon he had the same feelings as her, the same needs and wants. He was old, therefore wouldn't possibly understand her, but she couldn't be more wrong. Age was just a number. Age was just a body that withered, yet the mind was still young.

She'd learn.

The purr of a car engine came down the connection. She must be driving, or she'd pulled over to speak to him.

"William." He passed on his thoughts, already weary about the night going on longer than he'd anticipated. "So that's the long and short of it."

"I agree with you, he's a liability. Ring him. Tell him to come to the factory. Now. If he balks, say I'll be there. Tell him we've had a robbery. Make out the alarm wasn't set and that's how they got in."

"What do I tell him about why me and Ted are here? The issue he has is with Marlene, so telling him we're using her tonight… It gives him time to inform someone, like his wife or the police. If he thinks he's going to see a pile of minced person, he may well bottle it, despite your warning, and grass us up."

"Use your loaf. You were driving past and saw a light on." Cassie sighed. "How far along are you with Abbott?"

"Just about to fire Marlene up."

"Don't. I have a plan. Leave the body alone for now."

He waited for her to elaborate. She didn't. He should have known. She wasn't Lenny. She didn't trust them like he had.

Felix bit the bullet. "I was going to mention, and I don't want to step on toes, but Nathan's clothes."

"I'm at Handel Farm. I was off to the squat next. I'll be with you in a few. May as well collect William's clothes and do both at once after."

Silence met him, she'd cut the call, and Felix stared at Ted.

"She's wanting me to phone William. Get him here."

Ted shook his head. "Bollocks. I'm all for disposal, but getting involved in murder again... Lenny said we didn't have to do that anymore."

"But Lenny's not the boss."

Ted stood and rubbed his forehead. "Yep, definitely getting too old for this." He bent to drag Nathan upright.

"Leave him."

"Shit. She wants to test William?" Ted dropped the body like it was hot.

"I'd say so." Felix pulled up his contact list again and pressed William's name. It rang for ages, the man probably asleep. "He's not answering."

"He might switch his mobile off when he goes to bed. That's another black mark against him. Why can't people follow the fucking rules?"

"Is that a dig at me for phoning Cassie instead of texting?"

"No, your fuck-up is understandable. We've done it that way for years. Her chopping and changing that rule is a bit off if you ask me. It's like when them oven chips came out, remember? We were used to frying them, and the new way was confusing. Chips? In an oven?"

"What are you ruddy well on about?" The ringing in Felix's ear stopped, and he held a hand up to stop Ted explaining. He didn't really want to know about the fucking chips anyroad.

"Felix?" William sounded sleepy, confused, maybe dragged from a deep sleep where the world seemed alien when he'd woken up.

"Ay up, lad. We've got a problem at the factory. Some scrote's broken in, nicked a cow carcase. We saw lights on when we drove by."

William yawned. It seemed to go on for ages, and Felix resisted barking at him.

"Why haven't the police phoned me?" the manager whined.

"The alarm wasn't set. Cassie's aware."

"Shit. But I remember setting it because Sheryl and Pauline were gassing outside by the door, then they asked me about reducing their hours. Sheryl's got a granddaughter who needs looking after while her mam's at work, and Pauline's needing to take things steady because of her back."

Felix shrugged, not that William could see it. "Well then, it must have been disarmed, so it's an inside job."

"There's only us three and Cassie who have the code. Oh, and Joe. Francis."

"Are you accusing us?"

"No! Someone must have watched one of us putting the code in."

Felix raged on. "And Cassie and Francis would hardly steal their own goods, would they. Joe's no thief either. Look, she said for you to come down, Cassie did. You're the manager, so you need to deal with it."

"I'll phone the police now to save time."

Felix's heart rate jumped. *Why can't people do as they're fucking told? If Lenny were here, this little bastard wouldn't argue.* He remembered his own faux pas and blushed. "No, Cassie's sorted that. Get a move on. We want to get ourselves home."

"Fine. See you in fifteen minutes."

Felix pocketed his phone and jerked his head at Ted. "We'll wait outside."

"What's the situation with William?"

"He went on about phoning the police. All right, that's standard, but not in this instance."

Felix led the way, smiling at the sound of the side room door clicking shut, concealing Nathan from view. William would get a shock once it opened again and he was met with the sight of a bloodied corpse. While Felix and Ted didn't get

360

involved in murder these days, he had to admit the old thrill of an upcoming death was welcome. He hadn't felt so alive in years.

Out the back, they stood in the thinning snow, the wind tossing it about this way and that, reminding Felix of winters as a nipper. He'd grown up in Yorkshire, where the snow rested its icy head on the land more often than it did here, and he missed tobogganing down the slopes of Farmer Braithwaite's fields with Ted, their laughter left behind at the top of the hill along with their initial whoops of joy.

Where had the time gone?

His eyes stung, and he snapped them shut to block the tears. He didn't do getting sentimental and cursed the snow for bringing back memories. "Fucking weather." He viewed Ted through a misty lens.

"Hmm." Ted lifted his shoulders, dipped his chin. "Seen many a season, haven't we. Together."

"Wouldn't be without you. Wouldn't change a thing."

"Except maybe what's going to happen in the next fifteen minutes."

"Yep, there is that, although part of me might enjoy it. You know, it'll be like we're young again, helping Lenny."

Headlights appeared through the trees to the right on the main road. Cassie speeding here, Felix would bet. William was probably making a bloody coffee to drink on the way over. He was one of *those* types, the new breed who couldn't live without the stuff.

The lights vanished with the car heading along the front of the property, then came the crackle of tyres on the gravel driveway, the sound changing to whispers of frost-addled grass being flattened. Cassie's car appeared, and she parked beside the row of large wheelie bins and got out.

"Who's that?" Felix muttered, his guard up.

The blonde woman walked to the boot, her outfit all black, and she lifted the lid. Closed it. Came to stand before them holding a handle with a chain of…was that barbed wire? The light from the corridor behind spilt out, spotlighting her wheat-like hair, a riot of plaits, and her black-framed glasses.

"Cassie?" Ted huffed out air. "What the fucking Nora are you wearing a wig and specs for?"

"It's something I'm trying out. A disguise. Did it work?"

"Until I had a closer look, yes," Ted said.

"That's good enough for me." Cassie shrugged.

"What do you need one of them for? A disguise, I mean." Felix couldn't get over how the colour and style of hair could change a person so much. Like Ted had said, until she'd come closer and his brain had caught up, Felix had thought she was someone else.

"For reasons."

"That your new weapon, is it?" Felix nodded at the thing. Now he had a chance to look at it properly, he copped an eyeful of flesh attached to the barbs.

"Hmm." Cassie turned at the growl of another car. "He's come in from the other way."

Felix nodded. He hadn't seen any new headlights through the trees either. "Gone to McDonald's drive-through for one of their coffees, no doubt."

"Hardly the sort of man we need then," she said. "Like, his first thought should have been getting here immediately."

"I don't want to speak out of line, but I will." Felix sighed. "Your dad was wrong to think William was a safe bet."

"You're right." Cassie dragged the wig off and, on the way back to her car, removed the glasses. She tossed them onto the passenger seat then rejoined them, finger-combing her red locks with her free hand, the chain of barbed wire swaying in the other.

Felix shivered now he knew what had created Nathan's wounds.

William's car rounded the corner, and he parked beside Cassie's motor. He exited, takeaway coffee cup in hand, and approached, all floppy hair and flighty attitude. It was a mistake employing a Swindon man, and although he'd been living up north since his teens, he still wasn't a true Nottinghamshire lad. He'd picked up the dialect, but that was about all that was northern about him.

"Sorry, needed a brew to wake me up." William's laugh...it was forced, as if he were afraid.

As he should be. I wonder if he kissed his wife goodbye while she slept, told her he loved her. He'll never get the chance to do that again if he fucks up inside the factory.

"Not an acceptable answer," Cassie snapped. "Indoors. Now."

"I'm sorry, okay? Really."

She waited for William to enter, then followed him. Felix went next, leaving Ted to lock up—and lock up he would, barring the door so William couldn't escape easily, stalled by the bolts. Felix felt sorry for the chap, a bit, but loose lips and all that. This man wasn't going to keep quiet regarding Marlene for long, and tonight was about self-preservation for Felix, Ted, and Cassie. They had to protect themselves against getting caught, and all because Lenny had made a bad judgement call, Cassie carrying it out.

Unusual for Lenny to balls anything up.

It wasn't only those three who'd cop it. The Barrington was home to many a scally who worked for Cassie. They'd get arrested, too. Cassie had a duty to ensure that didn't happen. Taking a fella out to prevent that was par for the course. *If* that was what she chose to do.

"This way," Cassie said.

She entered the side room, and William glanced at Felix, his expression that of: *Fuck, we're going in there? With Marlene?*

Felix nodded, bracing for William to leg it, to push past him then Ted, rushing to the locked door, scrabbling to draw the bolts across.

William stepped inside. "Oh my fucking God."

Felix chuckled darkly, as did Ted behind him. Felix entered, then Ted did the same and closed the door, leaning on it. Cassie stood beside Nathan, William at the dead man's feet, and Felix stopped next to the southern-born prat.

"Christ, did the robbers kill him?" William darted his gaze to the mincer, and things slotted into place, going by the drop of his jaw and his eyes widening. "No. Oh no. I want nothing to do with this." He took a pace backwards, hands held high.

"Are you saying you won't follow orders?" Cassie asked. She looked at Felix and gestured for him to move away.

Felix reversed to the door and positioned himself beside his cousin who breathed heavily, fists clenched at his sides as though he geared himself up to witness their new boss in action.

"I'm not helping you put that man in the mincer," William spluttered. "Fucking hell, no."

"Are you sure?" Cassie tilted her head.

"I'm going to the police. I'm telling them about this mad shit." William took a step back.

Cassie raised her arm, and the barbed whip connected with William's face, the end curling around his head and sticking into his scalp. William screamed, raising his hands to his cheeks, attempting to peel the barbs off, his fingers and palms getting pierced.

"Let me help you there." Cassie took hold of the very end—no barbs there, as if she'd made it that way for this reason—and walked around

William to remove the spikes from the back. At the front, she snatched it off, a thick piece of skin going flying and landing on the side of Marlene's steel chute.

"Stone me," Ted whispered. "He's fucked."

William's screams continued, as did Cassie's assault on his face, until the man's features were obliterated, a mash of flesh and blood. He staggered to rest against the wall, the front of his top covered in scarlet. Cassie let her whip fly again, wrenching it away with such force his top lip ripped off, exposing gums, bloodied teeth, a macabre grimace beneath a wrecked nose and eyes that bled tears of torture.

The meat factory manager slid down the wall, his arse hitting the floor, a ghastly thud that churned Felix's stomach. William veered sideways, landing on the piece of lip, his body resting in the shape of a forty-five-degree angle, lifting his hands to cover his barb-minced face. A blood-speckled Cassie dropped the whip and straightened him out, straddled him, shifting the whimpering man onto his back. She sat on his torso, gloved hands around his crimson-drenched throat, and squeezed.

Fuck, it's Lenny all over again.

"This," she snarled. "This is what happens to people who don't play by my rules. Lenny doesn't run the show now, I do, and I won't have some prick threatening my business, my loyal employees. They don't deserve to go down because you opened your gob."

William raised his hands to grip her wrists, but the whip attack and blood loss had left him weak. Felix had a mind to step in, to stop this, but Ted stayed him with a hand on his arm.

"We don't want bullet holes in here," Ted whispered. "Leave her to work through her grief, her ascension. Let her do what she needs to, then things will calm down."

Felix wasn't so sure about that, not with the glint in her eyes, the madness sparkling in them. Cassie Grafton had stepped over a line Lenny had never crossed by using that whip, and it wasn't right.

"She's the new boss with her own rules," Ted murmured as the light went out of William's eyes. "And we've got to adapt to the change." He paused. "Or meet the same fate."

Chapter Twenty-Five

Two Weeks Later

Brenda snuggled up to Vance in his deceased mother's double bed, the fusty quilt cover stinking of unwashed bodies. It'd been a bit weird, shagging him there, in the place Wanda had died, but she'd tossed that oddness out of her head to give him the fuck of his life. Well, the eighth fuck of his life, considering she'd given him that many services since she'd turned up on his doorstep for the first time in years.

All afternoon and evening they'd talked, that day of the funeral, her apologising for not seeing they were destined to be together, begging him to forgive her, wheedling her way back into his affections, breaking down the steel wall he'd built between them when she'd ditched him.

He had forgiven her now, obviously, and if she continued to play her cards right, she'd get left all of his worldly goods once he snuffed it, let alone the usual cash withdrawal. She'd hand that over to Cassie, as per the rules, but the rest once probate was over? The bungalow and the money Wanda had bequeathed him? All Brenda's.

Vance had melted quite nicely, thanks, segueing into her care and allowing her to do her fake job as well as jump into his bed. It hadn't taken long, a couple of days, and she had him in the palm of her hand, especially as she hadn't complained about the tit-sucking palaver. At first, he'd only hinted they should get married, as soon as, so he'd finally get his wish before he departed this life, a woman who'd never deny him, whatever the chuff that meant. Brenda had acted shocked, mentioned the money, how it wasn't exactly fair she'd inherit everything, but he'd shoved that complaint aside.

And she'd smiled.

They'd applied for a license, and that was that.

It wasn't so bad having sex with Vance. As with all the other oldies, she shut her eyes and thought of nicer things, like Gucci shoes and expensive handbags, going through the motions, faking it so she could make it. And by God, she'd be well and truly making it this time. All that cash, and the bungalow must be worth a fair few bob an' all. She'd sell it, upgrade her own place, or maybe even buy one of the smaller properties on New Barrington. Who'd have thought she'd go *that* far up the ladder? It had been a dream of hers ever since the new builds had gone up, although they weren't so new now, but a dream was all she'd thought it would be.

Now, it was a distinct reality. So close she could taste it.

You've landed on your feet here, Brenda.

Vance snored. Bless. She'd worn him out. Another two weeks, and they'd be husband and wife at the end of a small registry office ceremony with Cassie and Francis as witnesses—Cassie had been made up about the news but cautioned it should be done on the quiet to stop any gossips spreading their foul suspicions. But those suspicions would be right, not that Brenda gave a shit. She'd become rich by any means necessary, even marrying a withered old man with a just-as-withered old dick.

She had her dress already, a flouncy number with all the frills and ruffles of a fabric meringue. She didn't care, it was the only time she'd be wed, so she'd turn up in style. Her dreams had long since had such a gown in them, outdated by today's reckoning, but some things you held on to, didn't you, and no matter how daft she'd look in it by other people's standards, she'd feel a million pounds for one speck of time.

While Vance slept, Brenda got herself caught up, reminding herself of what had been going on lately outside her part in the Barrington business.

She'd met up with Cassie to discuss the Vance situation and sucked in the other gossip like neat voddy up a straw, which had sent her head as giddy as the alcohol would.

Two weeks had passed since Nathan Abbott had gone missing, and what a ding-dong that had created, everyone on the Barrington speculating as to why he'd fucked off. The collective estate dwellers were stupid, blinkered not to realise he'd been 'disappeared', but they believed the man had done just that, no Marlene in sight.

And as for William, the meat factory manager, he'd gone walkabouts an' all. Joe had taken over that role, a temporary measure until Cassie trusted someone else enough to offer them a job. Lou had said she could handle the pigs for a while.

Karen and Sharon had done the usual and sent out an emergency flyer, and Nathan's dad, old

Henry, knocked on doors asking if anyone had seen his son. The stupid prat hadn't put two and two together from reading the news in a previous *The Barrington Life*, telling all about Cassie's new weapon. It had been announced too close to Nathan's vanishing act for it not to be related. William's wife was just as thick, phoning the police to say he'd vanished from their bed, her asleep and knowing nothing about it until the morning.

Brenda wondered what had happened to his car, but Cassie didn't elaborate. It was gone, that was all Brenda needed to know, apparently.

As for those daft souls who swallowed cover stories… People believed what they wanted to believe, especially if it meant they slept soundly at night, and Brenda wasn't going to shine any light on reality, not when she'd been taken into

Cassie's confidence. That was a step up from the usual, and Brenda was quite chuffed Cassie had chosen her to talk to.

Jason had come round to Brenda's the night Nathan had gone missing and told her what the new weapon was. Brenda couldn't help but admire the woman. Good for her in forging her own path. Not so good for Jason, who admitted he was floundering in breaking Cassie down in his mission to scoop the estate for himself.

Once Vance died, Brenda would make it *her* mission to record Jason saying shit like that so she could play it to Cassie, making out she hadn't told her about his plans until then as she'd been gathering evidence, wanting to be sure he was plotting Cassie's downfall. That was a dangerous thing to do, keeping it from Cassie, but Brenda's wealth came first, and she'd be damned if some young girl's welfare would come between her and the cash.

Get through these two weeks, marry Vance, then give him such a vigorous workout he'll die like Michael.

You had to look after yourself, didn't you.

Vance stirred, mumbling and turning over. "Come on, littlun. Come to Uncle Vance."

Brenda's skin chilled, and her stomach churned. "What was that you said?" She spooned him, his rough, cheapo pyjamas abrading her naked body. They smelt as musty as the quilt. She made a mental note to wash it all tomorrow.

"Do as you're fucking told," Vance snapped. He sounded alert, awake, not drugged by sleep.

She jolted in shock.

"I haven't done anything for you to be barking at me like that, Vance bleedin' Johnson," she said, indignant. "What's got *your* goat?"

"You look good dead," he whispered. "So good."

Brenda pulled away, a sharp movement, rising on one elbow, her tongue losing all moisture. Something wasn't right and, nauseated, she got up and walked round to Vance's side of the bed. She knelt, debris from the carpet digging into her skin, and switched on the lamp. "*What* did you say?"

His eyes were closed, his breathing heavy. Talking in his sleep, was that it?

"Who looks good dead?" She dreaded the answer, if she'd even get one.

Vance flung himself over onto his back, arms up by his head, fingers twitching, playing an invisible piano. "That's it, by The Beast."

Brenda's mind went haywire. What the hell was he dreaming about? This was the first time she'd slept over so had no idea if he chattered in his sleep every night. She shook him, but he didn't wake, his eyelids flickering with REM, his life-weathered face tight with what she could only assume was anger, a grimace she didn't much like.

"You shouldn't have been out wandering," he muttered. "I wouldn't have killed you then. Wouldn't have had the *urge*."

It came out somewhat garbled, but she'd made the words out all right. He'd killed someone? Vance? No, she wouldn't believe it. He must be deep in one of those odd dreams. She got them sometimes, where she did things she'd never do while awake, and in the light of morning, she felt guilty for something she hadn't been able to control. The mind, it was a funny bugger.

"I kept it inside until you," he groused. "It's your fault I did what I did after. You set me off."

Brenda's frown hurt, and a throb set up behind her right eye. She'd get a migraine soon, that was always a warning.

"Vance, you're having one of them daft nightmares. Wake up." She poked and prodded him. "Who did you kill?" She held her breath, which was a silly thing to do, wasn't it? A dream wasn't his fault. He didn't have any influence over what he was saying. What he said if he answered her wouldn't *mean* anything.

"Jess," he hissed. "Jess."

Brenda sprang away from the bed, landing on her arse, her chest tight, legs splayed, her lady garden on display. She snapped her knees together and shook her head in disbelief, and in rapid-fire succession, things whipped into her mind, flashes of information one after the other, snapshots of time gone by.

Jess Wilson being snatched.

Her body found near The Beast.

Vance moving away afterwards, to Newcastle.

Him driving a lorry; Wanda had crowed about that in The Donny, her son a delivery man, and wasn't he a clever boy to snag such a good job?

Children going missing on the news, turning up dead the same as Jess in random parts of the country.

Every haulage driver questioned but no arrests made, a mystery as to who was committing such hideous crimes.

She stood on shaking legs, reversing away from him, hand raised to clutch her aching chest. She couldn't stay here, couldn't let him touch her anymore. Wouldn't get all his money. Couldn't marry a man who'd killed kiddies. And she knew he had, that it was him, not the ramblings of a man caught in the riptide depths of sleep.

Something intrinsically *knowing* seeped inside her, a viscous gloop spreading throughout until she got too hot and couldn't steady her breathing. Hyperventilating, she leant on the wall beside Wanda's hulking great walnut wardrobe and concentrated on the feel of the ancient, eighties stippled wallpaper beneath her hands. Something, anything to centre her. Anaglypta, it was called anaglypta. She pressed a fingertip to a pointed knobble and welcomed the pinch of pain.

But as she calmed, more information loaded into her brain, snatching her hold on the here and now, plunging her back into the past. The Mechanic. He'd kidnapped Jess, so Lenny had confided. Dave Colson was a kid killer.

Or was he? What if Vance had done that?

What if Lenny had murdered the wrong man?

No. Vance just said if she hadn't been out wandering…

Oh fuck, oh shit, had Jess got away from The Mechanic and Vance had intercepted? Why had he killed her? What possessed him to even *think* about doing that? Brenda understood the other kind of killing, the Lenny and Cassie and Jason kind, but this? No, she'd never get to grips with that.

In a panic, her lungs still refusing to work properly, she stumbled over to her discarded clothes on the floor and slung them on, her movements jerky and so full of fright she couldn't stand it. She grabbed her shoes and bag, rushing for the door, wrenching it open, light from the hallway spilling in, momentary blindness bleaching her eyeballs and—

"Where are you going?" Vance said, monotone.

Brenda halted, her free hand on the doorframe, knuckles white, fear keeping her immobile, and she stared at the living room door opposite. It was ajar, the coffee table visible beneath the light bulb encased in a manky amber glass shade, their empty wine goblets glinting, and she recalled her and Vance laughing, getting drunk before tumbling into bed.

In her mind, she refreshed where the front door was. At least this was a bungalow and she wouldn't have to contend with any stairs.

"I need a drink," she said. That was a good enough excuse, wasn't it?

She turned, expecting Vance to be staring at her, his eyes wide and glaring in accusation, thinking she was leaving him for good again, but he was still asleep, oh, thank Christ, he was still blessedly asleep. Who was he talking to in that dream? Jess? Had he asked that babby where she was going?

"Fucking hell no..." Brenda said on a shaky exhale.

Her imagination ran riot, and she saw it all, him approaching the toddler, giving her the once-over, seeing those sodding tiny wellies and the rainbow coat, deciding then and there he was going to kill her and leave her at the foot of The Beast in the rain, letting her get all wet, the poor mite.

Brenda made it to the front door and stopped to slip her stilettos on, overbalancing and crashing into the telephone table. She paused, waiting for the noise to wake Vance, but he shouted in his sleep, horrible words she'd never forget.

"Stop wriggling, you little bitch!"

Out, Brenda was out of that place and running down the garden path, crying and terrified for Jess, her death playing out inside the mind of a deviant bastard, one Brenda had known was off all those years ago but she hadn't been able to put her finger on exactly what it was.

Now she knew, and the only person she could rely on to sort this was Cassie.

Only a Grafton would dish out the punishment such a wretched creature deserved.

Chapter Twenty-Six

Cassie sighed at the bleep of her work phone. She sat at Dad's desk in the home office, writing her to-do list in code, a form of shorthand he'd taught her so if the house was raided by the police for any reason, they wouldn't understand what things said. Years of leatherbound volumes sat on the bookshelf and contained slights against him, good deeds, warnings, murders, the names of employees—both sides of the business—and all sorts pertaining to his working life. Each one was named INFORMATION at the tops of the spines with the years at the bottom, also in code.

A set of Grafton's Britannica.

Cassie had read them all, her way of getting to know the history of his reign on the Barrington, plus brushing up on the code. She didn't hope to remember all of it, but a lot had stuck.

Mam was in bed. Earlier, she'd cried behind her bedroom door, and it had set Cassie off to do the same. Hearing someone else's wrenching sobs would do that to you. They were distanced by grief and the wall between their rooms, but in her heart, Cassie held Mam close, hoping she sensed her comfort.

She rubbed her still-stinging eyes, picked up her phone, and read the message.

Brenda: *Problem.*

Great. Cassie sighed again and responded: *What sort?*

Brenda: *I think I should have rung you.*

So, a life-or-death situation.

Cassie: *Then why didn't you?*

Brenda: *Because the issue already happened so I was confused as to what to do.*

For fuck's sake. Had she shagged Vance to death? If so, this was becoming a bit of a habit. She needed to be more careful, especially when the money withdrawal hadn't been secured yet.

Cassie got up and took the RESIDENTS volume off the shelf, the only one she hadn't read from cover to cover. This she only browsed if she needed to look someone up if they'd pissed her off, and she could see where they were on warnings and whether they needed a final. That reminded her to add an addendum to Richie Prince's page that he was dead. Plus Nathan Abbott and William Dougherty.

It all fell to her now.

If only she could trust a secretary. She didn't want Mam having the hassle.

She flicked through the back pages, finding Vance Johnson to double-check there would be no comeback when he died. Brenda would have already known a lot about him, having been a resident since day dot, but something told Cassie to look anyroad. Brenda would have gone on what she knew from living on the estate, the 'just knowing him' version.

VANCE JOHNSON

DOB: June 5th 1949 – still alive

ADDRESS: 27 Newbold Avenue, on Old – now Newcastle, unknown: see note below

OCCUPATION: Lorry driver – EDIT: is he the nonce killing them kids? Suspect this, so if he returns to the Barrington, visit needed. If the truth comes out, final warning.

FAMILY: Mother, Wanda. EDIT: deceased. Father, Robert, deceased. No other relatives.

MISDEMEANOURS: June 2nd 1997 – fight with Joe Wilson. Reason: Vance touched Lou up in The Donny, saying, "Did you breastfeed?" Excuse: accidental brushing of hand on tit at bar; he'd said what he'd said as general conversation. Problem: Vance has 'accidentally' done this to Lou before. Twice. Fucking tosser.

WARNINGS: Punched for above incident by me, also threatened with a blade.

WATCH OUT FOR: Repeat of incident.

EDIT: July 1997: He's moved away. Keep an eye on any return to the patch.

AMENDMENTS: Vance back at Wanda's, Nov 2020. Visit complete. Innocent of my suspicions. The fella's come home to die. Get contacts to confirm his story. Trevor to take over with Brenda. Two targets on the go? (Vance and Michael Peg.)

Cassie frowned. Dad must have kept an eye on people even when they left the area. And if he suspected Vance was a child killer, which children did he mean? And how come Brenda hadn't worked the two targets at once like Dad had mentioned? Maybe the contacts hadn't come through with Vance's information in time, then Michael had died the same day as Dad so…

Brenda: *You've gone quiet.*

Cassie: *Was looking something up. Meet me by The Beast.*

Brenda: *Oh fuck. Okay.*

What was that all about, the 'oh fuck'? Was something already happening there? Had angry Barringtons gathered for a fight or whatever and things had got out of hand? Why hadn't Karen or Sharon phoned with that info? Wasn't the grassvine bloody working?

Cassie: *Do I need to bring my new weapon? Jason? Some heavyweights?*

Brenda: *No. Just you.*

Cassie: *Something feels off. What are you up to?*

Brenda: *Nowt! I need to talk without ears.*

Cassie: *Okay.*

Cassie left the office and opened the cupboard in the hallway, taking out her boots and coat. She slipped them on, thinking to walk to The Beast seeing as it was only a couple of streets away, then changed her mind because of the cold—plus, she may well need her weapon anyroad, and she stored that in the locked briefcase in the boot. Dad would brain her if he were alive, saying you couldn't trust anyone in the daytime let alone in the darkness, so the car it was.

Gun on the passenger seat just in case, she drove off. So she was away from home, she parked in the closest street to The Beast on Old Barrington, tucking the vehicle down the side of someone's house, thinking they wouldn't mind, seeing as their lights were off, and if they did mind, they could bugger off. Briefcase in one hand, gun by her side in the other, she walked down the alley. At the end, she scanned the area—houses opposite, some with lights on, no one around. She headed across the grass expanse that separated Old from New and moved to the stone sculpture. It was lit by an automatic solar lamp so Jess' memory was alive in sunshine and darkness, always there to remind people that if they broke the Barrington law, they'd get found out and disposed of, like Jess's killer had.

She hated this stone creature which couldn't make its mind up if it were a horse or something else, and shuddered at the flared nostrils, the popping-with-fear eyes, the way it seemed as if it'd come to life any second and trample her.

Nerves steadied, she stepped over one of the chains cordoning it off and, at the plinth, stared at where her toddler friend had been dumped, thinking herself lucky that *she* hadn't been snatched, too. Dad had said she could well have been if The Mechanic wanted enough money for a second round of private IVF, and she shuddered at how scared she'd have been, how she'd have wanted Mam and Dad, how she'd have cried for them.

Cassie shut the emotions down and concentrated on watching for Brenda. The sound of a car had her turning to the first row of homes on New Barrington, their fronts facing The Beast. They were a hotchpotch sight, some slim and tall, others stout and short, as though the planners hadn't come to an agreement on the dominant style for that road.

Brenda must have had the same thought about driving away from home and parked outside a narrow three-storey property on New. She opened the driver's door, the interior light splashing onto her face for a brief enough moment that Cassie clocked the worry in her features, albeit from a few metres away, but the frown was definitely there.

What the hell had happened?

Cassie immediately checked for passengers, for the hunched shape of someone hiding in the back seat. She trusted Brenda, despite her being good buddies with Karen Scholes, but it didn't hurt to be sure. As far as she could see, no one else occupied the vehicle.

Brenda got out and closed the door, the blip of her locks engaging loud above the moaning of the abrupt wind that added to the ominous dread creeping into Cassie. She waited for the woman to make her way across the grass in her high heels, cock a leg over a chain, and come to her.

"What's going on?" Cassie asked, voice low. The wind lifted her lowered hood and pushed it against the back of her head.

"It's Vance. He was having a nightmare."

Irritation spiked. Was that it? Cassie had been called out in this shitty weather to hear about Vance's *sleeping* habits? "And?"

"He was…he was talking about Jess."

"Jess?" Cassie didn't know any other Jess apart from… "Jessica *Wilson*?"

A pause. A frantic nod. "I think…I think he killed her."

All the air left Cassie in a rush. She sucked more in, giving herself time to think on what Brenda had said. *Vance* had killed Jess, not The Mechanic? If so, how the hell had Dad got it so wrong? Years later, he'd told her about his visit to Dave Coulson and had sworn the man was guilty. He'd admitted to taking her, after all. And she'd read about it in one of the volumes. Earlier, when she'd read the RESIDENTS book, it hadn't specified which kids Dad suspected Vance of killing, and besides, he'd recently cleared him in November.

"What did he say?" Cassie gripped the gun tight and lowered the weapon case to the ground.

If Vance were in front of her now, she'd snap the fucking lid open and whip the bastard.

Brenda told her story, and by the end of it, she was crying, staring at the place where Jess had been found, her bottom lip trembling. "That's why he left the area, it had to have been. He'd applied for a job away from here on purpose. I bet he heard about what had happened to The Mechanic, the real reason he went missing, you know how whispers get round, and he shit himself."

"I was thinking along the same lines. Dad got rid of The Mechanic, and Vance took his chance to get out of here."

"D'you know what's always bothered me? Okay, New Barrington wasn't built back then, but those houses over there on the edge of Old... Why didn't someone see him dropping Jess off

403

here? It was summer, Karen had delivered *The Life* and walked this way, and no one had been on the grass like usual. Kids always played here, for fuck's sake. Climbed The Beast. Why…?" She sighed.

"Dad said it had been raining, all that week it was awful, so people wouldn't have been out and about."

"Ah, I recall that now."

Cassie didn't want to go down an alley called Memory Lane, one she'd never witnessed. That was in Brenda's head, in her heart, not something Cassie could remember. She changed the subject. "What did you mean about the other children?" Although she now had an idea.

"I thought about it after Vance had babbled. It was all over the news. You won't remember because you were little. But these toddlers, they were taken from public places like shopping

404

centres or their front gardens while they were playing, and no one saw who did it. He was never caught on CCTV. The police, they didn't know where to turn. It had to have been him. He was a fucking lorry driver. Ample opportunity to kidnap and kill. The Yorkshire Ripper, except he killed nippers not women. God, he could be one of those sick fuckers who based himself on him."

So Dad's initial suspicions were right? Vance must have spun him a convincing line for Dad to let him off.

"Surely the police would have sussed it was him if they'd spoken to all the drivers like you told me." Cassie pushed away the thought that she was playing Devil's advocate so it meant Dad hadn't made a mistake.

"That's what I thought, but what if he did his usual deliveries then went a few miles away to take kids? Like, the next day even, after he'd parked up in a lay-by to sleep or whatever."

"That's speculation."

"But he must have done something like that. The evidence is too great to be a coincidence. Jess, him leaving, the other kids being done over."

Cassie bristled. There was no time to gas about the past. "You left him asleep in bed, you said."

Brenda nodded. "I couldn't stay in there. Couldn't stand being near him."

"I get that. But we're going to have to go back, you know that, don't you. We can't let this slide." *I have to fix what Dad didn't finish.*

Brenda fussed with the zip of her pink fleece top. Where was her coat? Had she legged it from Vance's without it, or was it in the car? Christ, she must be freezing. Or maybe the heat of truth had her warm enough to stand this bone-freezing weather.

"What will we do, torch it like Michael's?" Brenda turned her head to stare at Cassie. "It should be okay; the bungalows are all detached. I doubt anyone will notice it's on fire, they'll all be asleep."

"We could do, but not with Vance inside. He needs taking to the squat."

"Can't Jason do that?"

"No. We'll do it. Between you and me, I can't stand Dad's memory being tarnished, and it will be, because he muffed right up on this."

Brenda wrung her hands. "But what about Trevor? He's going to ask where Vance has gone, why I'm not going to his house every day. He's my handler, he needs to know what I'm doing. He'll *expect* to know."

"I'm the boss, and Trevor will know only what I want him to."

"But Lenny—"

Cassie told herself not to scream. "I swear to God, if someone says that one more time... Lenny is *dead*, Brenda. *I'm* here. *I'm* the one left to mop up this kind of shite. And if Dad had done his due diligence properly, he would have known someone else killed Jess. Okay, The Mechanic admitted to taking her, but he said he didn't murder the kid. The great Lenny Grafton didn't listen, he knew best." Cassie slapped her forehead with the heel of her free hand. "For fuck's *sake*, Dad." She stared at the starless sky, at the heavy clouds obscuring them. "What have you done?"

Brenda rested a hand on Cassie's. "Deep breath, duck. I'm sorry, I've gone and got you all riled up. Of course we'll fix this. For Jess. For Joe and Lou."

"Joe…" Cassie groaned at what the outcome could be if she went with her instincts. The fallout. More people to keep their mouths shut. Someone else in the business definitely knowing because she'd given Joe the job of managing the meat factory. But there was justice to be had. She made a final decision. "Joe and Lou should be there."

"Oh my Lord…" Brenda thumped her arse down on the plinth, a whoosh of air coming out of her. The beam from the solar light positioned half a metre ahead gave the illusion she was a lonely ghost keeping vigil.

Cassie shivered. "They can at least have the option. If they find out I went ahead without them… This is their *child* we're talking about."

"But what if Vance tells them what he did?" Brenda whispered. "Can they handle the truth?

He said…he said, 'Stop wriggling, you little bitch!' What was he *doing* to her, Cass? What the *fuck* did that little one go through?"

Emotion formed a ball in Cassie's throat. "I don't know, and I'm not sure I want to." She sighed and tucked her gun in the waistband of her jeans. Pulled her phone from her pocket. Dialled Joe.

He answered quickly. "Ay up, Cassie. Everything all right?"

"No, it isn't. I won't go around the houses. I'm so sorry, but I know who really killed Jess."

"*What*?" A rush of breath filtered down the line. "It wasn't The Mechanic?"

"Not from what I've heard, no."

"Jesus Christ…"

"What's happened?" Lou asked him the background.

Cassie imagined the poor woman clutching at the neck of her cardigan. "Up to you if you tell her. And up to you if you want to make your way over to the squat in about an hour."

"Hang on, Lou, give me a second," Joe said. Then to Cassie, "You've got him? It *is* a 'he', isn't it?"

"I'm on my way to the house now, and yes, it's a he. You're in for a shock when you find out who it is, fair warning and all that."

"Shit. Someone I know?"

"Yeah. Give me half an hour to collect him. Brenda's with me."

"Right. Right. Okay."

"Drive carefully."

"I will."

Cassie swiped her screen and slid the phone back into her pocket. She picked up her weapon case. "He's coming by the sounds of it. Don't know about Lou."

Brenda stood, shoulders slumped. "We'll miss out on the cash withdrawal. I'm sorry."

"Fuck the money." Cassie straightened her spine. "Some things are more important."

But she wasn't sure if she meant avenging Jess's death or covering up Lenny Grafton's botch job.

Chapter Twenty-Seven

Vance's bungalow stood as a blot on the landscape beside its neighbours, the garden overrun with winter weeds that choked the bases of the hedges surrounding the square of lengthy grass, all shown in their tatty glory beneath the harsh light streaming out through the

413

fingerprint-smeared living room window. The curtains were open, and Cassie walked over and stared through at the old-fashioned furniture: a brown velour sofa, tile-topped coffee table, and a wooden wall unit full to bursting with a lifetime of knick-knacks that meant nothing to anyone but Wanda and Vance Johnson. Dusty china birds, a creepy array of clean glass angels, grubby vases, paperweights, and numerous teapots in various shapes: cottages, animals, even a lighthouse.

Cassie remembered Wanda as a withered old woman no matter how many years passed; she'd always looked the same. She'd sunk gin after gin in The Donny even when she'd progressed to needing a Zimmer. As a child, Cassie had grown up amongst the Barrington lot, her extended family to be found in the pub whenever Dad had taken her there, the trip made with her high on his shoulders, queen of the world, the sun or rain on her face. Vance, now he'd been the sort of man Mam had veered away from, she'd said something to that effect recently after Cassie had told her he was Brenda's latest mark.

"Looked at you funny, up and down, like." Mam had shuddered as if his gaze had been on her there and then. "Had a thing about tits. There was something up with him, but I couldn't figure out what."

Now Cassie knew why. If his sleepy ramblings were to be believed, he was a killer, of children no less, and a woman was bound to sense that, a mother anyroad, her senses primed to sniff out anyone who'd potentially harm her brood. How many had gathered their kids to the safety of their skirts if he'd been around, unable to understand why they'd done it? How many would twig now if they knew what he'd done, understanding that inborn knowledge that Vance was a bad man, an unspoken 'feeling' that pushed them to protect?

"Have you got a key?" Cassie whispered to Brenda on her way back to the doorstep, glad to be away from the weird stares of the glass angels. They all had eyes that seemed to have been painted on, cut-in-half boiled eggs on clear faces.

"Yeah. Hang on." Brenda dug a hand in her bag and produced a bunch. She selected the correct one and inserted it into the Yale. Twisted. Paused. Gazed at Cassie, swallowing. "What if he's awake?"

"What of it?" Cassie lifted her hand in front of her so it was shielded from anyone nosing out of their windows, her gun held tight.

Brenda gasped. "But someone will hear the shot."

"Do you think I was born yesterday? I won't be using it, just getting him to do what I want by pointing it at him."

Brenda took a deep breath and entered, Cassie close behind. Brenda snatched a fur-collared black coat off the newel post and put it on, then trotted down the hallway. Her heels had dirt at the bottoms where they must have pierced the hard ground by The Beast. She stopped at an open door and peered in. Even from the side view of her face, Cassie knew the woman hated what she saw. Probably hated herself for shagging the baby-killing bastard an' all. But she hadn't known who he really was so couldn't be blamed for that.

"He's still out for the count," Brenda whispered.

Cassie stepped in front of her and stared at the wanker in the bed. Acute rage propelled her into the room to stand beside him. She glared down at an old man who appeared like any other innocent grandad, sleeping away the creaks and aches of the day. She looked around, spying a dressing gown belt draped over a ladderback dining chair in the corner, its companion piece in a heap on the floor. Her mind zipped back to Doreen grabbing a pair of tights to use in place of hers. Cassie shook the thought off and picked up the belt, then poked into an open drawer of a tall chest and removed a balled-up pair of dark-grey socks.

Gun in her waistband, she moved back to the bed and carefully lifted one of Vance's hands, both flung up by his head. She fed the belt beneath it and did the same with the other one. Slow and steady, she drew the lengths of belt over each other as if tying them, getting ready to do

418

just that in one quick move in case he woke and struggled. She managed it, then repeated the tying process so it formed a tight knot, all while Vance stirred, mumbled, and tried to part his pressed-together wrists. Cassie gripped the ends of the belt and yanked him upright.

He opened his eyes and gawked at her, blinking, maybe thinking he was still in that wretched dream with Jess, confused as to why a new participant stood there, someone he wouldn't recognise as he'd been away for so long. Unless he'd been watching since his November return, getting reacquainted with the residents.

"Who the fuck are you?" He fought the bonds.

"I'm your worst bloody nightmare," she said. "I'm all your pigeons coming home to roost at once. I'm maybe the last face you'll see in your disgusting life."

He opened his mouth to protest, and she stuffed the socks inside, wedging them deep, the movement throwing him back down to the mattress. His eyes bulged, vehement spite in them, and she slapped his wrinkled cheek, unable to hold back her monster's rage any longer. He let out a muffled cry, but any remorse she'd usually have for striking an elderly gentleman wasn't present, and gentleman was a grand term for one so despicable.

She leant over, staring straight at him. "And to answer your question properly, I'm Cassie Grafton, here to make sure you pay for what you did to Jessica Wilson—and those other children you murdered."

He glowered, and she knew, without any doubt whatsoever, that he'd killed them all, that Dad had made a hideous error of judgement. She gripped his hair and wrenched him, dragging him off the bed and across towards the door. He was heavy for someone so slight, so she fisted a chunk of his pyjama top and hauled him to Brenda, holding his top half up by his scruff and hair, his spindly legs splayed on the floor, poking through the ruched-up hems of his cheap pyjamas.

"Punch him," Cassie said. "Go on, punch the fucker's lights out. Get all that anger out of you before we move on to the next step."

Brenda gazed down at Vance, the keys still in one hand, and she pushed a long one between two fingers, the type that resembled a lock pick. She tightened her grip into a fist, the jagged-edged key poking out, and drew her arm back and up.

"I hate you," she said. "I fucking knew something was off about you."

And she let her fist fly downwards, the key sinking into one of Vance's widened eyes.

Cassie smiled at the muffled scream fighting to be heard around the socks. The blood. The eye coming out on the end of the key, gloop following it, Brenda breaking the connection off and holding that eyeball up in the light of the landing.

They both started at it, ignoring Vance writhing and grunting on the shitty carpet, having some kind of shivering fit.

"Payback has begun," Cassie said. "And fuck me will it be a bitch."

Chapter Twenty-Eight

Outside their farmhouse, Joe stared across from the driver's seat at Lou. "Are you sure you—"

"I'm sure." She nodded, perhaps convincing herself. "We didn't get a chance to take our anger out on The Mechanic, so if this other fucker's the one who really killed our girl, I want to watch him die, get minced, and fed to the pigs."

"Can you handle it? You know, the guilt, afterwards?"

"Guilt? I can handle *anything* after losing a child. *Nothing* is as bad as that. There's no guilt to be had here, not when it comes to our Jess." Lou held the throw blanket around herself tighter, the squares of the tartan turning into rectangles where it had folded.

Joe started the engine, set the heater on high so she could warm up, and drove around the farmhouse and onto the driveway. He'd been tired before Cassie had rung, from running a farm he hadn't wanted in the first place plus taking over the managerial role at the meat factory. All right, that was temporary, but he was the ideal candidate as he'd worked alongside Lenny at the beginning and knew every inch of the place. Lou had taken on more jobs at the farm, and her nephew, Ben, conveniently unemployed, had come to help her out.

Selfishly, Joe reckoned it was a good situation—he got away from the heavy jobs at the farm and was back in the belly of a factory he'd always loved working in. After this…whatever it was tonight…he'd chat to Lou and suggest they keep Ben on and Joe could stay at the factory. The only thing Ben wouldn't know about was the contents of Marlene's belly feeding the pigs. Maybe, if Cassie still wanted a new manager, Joe could share the job with whoever it was or at least show them the ropes for a bit.

Wide awake from the adrenaline rush, he navigated the empty country road.

"How did Lenny miss this?" Lou asked. "How come he was convinced it was The Mechanic? I trusted him, thought he'd done the job. And how come Cassie's discovered who it really was? Has she been going through those weird books of Lenny's and making sure things to do with his reign don't come back to bite her on the arse?"

"She's with Brenda, so maybe she told her?"

It was frustrating not knowing who it was. If he did, he'd be able to tie things together, remember any incidents involving the man. He could scan his memory to see if anything glaring had happened back then, something *he'd* also missed. And Lou. If The Mechanic had snatched Jess, had the person in the back of the van killed their little girl? Was that who they were going to meet? Lenny hadn't found out who that was, and no amount of probing on Joe's part had revealed anything either.

"Brenda?" Lou said. "The one who shags the old men?"

Joe nodded, heading to the farther outskirts. Of course Lou knew about the business. Lenny had been Joe's best mate, they'd continued to go round there for dinner throughout the years, and business was inevitably discussed, although Joe doubted Lenny had told him everything. Francis was a leaning post for Lou, so she'd have talked things through, and Lou had a macabre thing about watching Cassie grow up so she could see what Jess would have done at each stage of development. *Was* it macabre, though, or natural?

"Yes," he said. "Brenda brings in quite a bit of revenue with her little scheme."

"I know, I was just checking which Brenda it was, because there's that other one who works in Wilko. Who's she working with now? Which old man?"

"No idea."

"I thought Lenny told you things."

"Some, not all."

The squat came into view, a dark shape on the near horizon, a lonely one folks ignored as an abandoned property, and those who did maybe ponder on it while driving past probably grumbled at the waste, how a family ought to fill it, bring it back to life, their laughter seeping into the walls.

His stomach cramped—shit, did he really want to know who it was? Part of him did, no doubt about it. Putting the past properly to bed and accepting they'd found the man in the back of the van—as Joe suspected—meant they could move on that little bit more. But another part wanted nothing to do with it, especially because Cassie had said he knew the fella.

Was it someone he'd interacted with since Jess's murder? Someone who'd spoken to him,

428

joked with him in The Donny, bought him a *pint*, for fuck's sake? Had he been laughing all this time, congratulating himself that he'd got away with it, his part in the snatch undetected, Joe, the dumb father, totally unaware?

"Should we do this?" he said. "Do we really want to torment ourselves even more?"

Lou shrugged off the blanket and gripped her hair at the sides. "How can you *say* that? For *years* we've wondered who the other person was. Tortured ourselves with whether we've walked past him on the fucking market or in Sainsbury's. Whether we're drinking from the same glasses he's used in the pub. At least I have. Those are the sorts of things that go round inside my head. Every. Single. Day. The what-ifs will kill me. Now we have a chance to put things right."

"I'm sorry." Joe felt all kinds of bastard. "I was just thinking of you, that's all." *And yourself, you lying wanker.* He was afraid. Of what he'd feel. Of the rage. Of finally breaking completely.

Of *knowing*.

He took the turning and drove up the squat's driveway. Many a man and a few women had died here within these decrepit walls. People came and cleaned up any mess, removing the presence of those murdered, not only in the squat but from this town, by filtering whispers to those on the Barrington that so-and-so had up and left, never to come back. Sometimes Marlene was mentioned, other times not, depending on what message Lenny had wanted to convey.

What would Cassie want to do in this instance? Keep it quiet? Would she want to let everyone know her father had got it so wrong? That he'd dropped the massive ball he'd always bragged he could keep up in the air?

Joe parked around the back between Cassie's and Brenda's cars, his gut in a knot, and shut the engine off. He reached out and took Lou's hand. "When this is done, we don't talk of it outside the farmhouse. We were never here. Tonight, we were in bed, asleep."

"I know enough about the Grafton way to realise that, Joe, I'm not stupid."

He forgave her for the snippy tone. It was understandable, after all. "I'm protecting you, that's why I said it."

"Thank you. I'm sorry. It's just…"

He squeezed her fingers. "We've come to the end."

"It'll never be the end. Not in here." Lou tapped her chest. "Or in here." She poked a finger at her head a bit too hard. "What that man did will never go away. Not for me. It'll follow me like it always has done."

Joe took a deep breath. "Come on, my lovely. Let's see what's what."

He got out of the car and walked around to open Lou's door, but she'd already exited, closing it nice and quiet, the tartan blanket left inside. He linked arms with her, his somewhat fragile wife at times, yet others she was a lioness, hunting for the truth, wanting bloodshed. Tonight she was the lioness, it seemed. She shrugged him off and went ahead, turning the handle on the front door and marching inside.

He rushed after her, wanting to protect her every step of the way.

"Cass?" she called out.

"In the living room."

Lou headed there while Joe shut the front door. He turned to follow her, stopping short at the sight of his woman standing in the living room doorway, lips parted, tears shining in her eyes.

"You?" she whispered. *"You?"*

Chapter Twenty-Nine

Anaked Vance couldn't get away from the woman advancing on him. She hadn't aged well, he could tell that even with the use of only one eye. He'd still touch her tits given half the chance, though, those balloons of flesh that reminded him of childhood, where he'd sucked at his mother's until he was six years old.

That strange little thought—strange considering the circumstances—flitted away, and survival took its place.

He braced for impact.

"You fucking *bastard*!" Lou Wilson came at him, fingers curled into claws, arms raised. Her face bore the evidence of her rage, her grief, her utter hatred for him.

Just like Wanda. They were *all* like Wanda.

His wrists were tied behind him, around the back of a paint-spattered dining chair, his ankles roped to the front legs, and there was no way of defending himself. That Cassie bitch had informed him it was no more than he deserved, a beating from the woman who'd birthed Jess Wilson, denied the chance to see her little girl grow up. Denied the love, the bonding as her child went from toddler to child to teenager to woman.

The laughter, the tears, the everything.

Lou slapped at him, then punched, screeching, and he suffered the onslaught—with dignity, he reckoned, not uttering a sound despite his eye socket banging with pain. He didn't have the socks in his mouth anymore, Cassie removing them to question him earlier, and he hadn't said anything except to admit he'd murdered Jess, his hands around her throat, sitting on her legs to stop them from kicking while the breath left her small body, and how the child had struggled.

Cassie had restraint, as did Brenda. They hadn't touched him, not like this woman was. Lou grabbed his hair and wrenched it out— another round of agony—standing there in front of him, her magnificent chest rising and falling, handfuls of his grey strands draped between her slim fingers. She'd lost all that baby weight, going back to the slender form she'd paraded around the estate years ago, prior to meeting Joe, her jugs still nice and firm. Big. Vance had lusted after her, admired her breasts, wishing he could suck them, receive the same feeling he'd had as a child from a mother, one that had vanished the moment Wanda fucking Johnson had cut off her milk supply, saying he was too big to have any more.

Abandoned, that's what he'd been without his source of comfort, and as a growing man, he'd become obsessed with touching what he'd been denied. He'd snuck a couple of feels off Lou in his time, but Lenny had ruined it all by punching him, then warning him off with that poxy knife of his. Brenda hadn't liked him pawing at her, and he supposed that was why she'd left him.

Lou dropped his hair and lunged forward. Her nails scraped down his cheeks, and she was that close her chest was within touching distance. If only his wrists weren't tied. He grunted in anger, at being refused what he coveted most, *again*, and her fist connecting with his empty eye socket sent a boom of pain through his head. She punched him over and over, a creepy screech barrelling through her skewed lips. The chair toppled, and he thumped to the floor, his temple whacking it, a bone in his arm breaking from being squashed between the carpet and the wood of the chair.

He screamed then, hating himself for it. White-hot pain penetrated his arm, but he had no strength left to attempt flipping the chair onto its back.

Lou stepped away, out of breath, tears streaming, and satisfaction wended through

Vance. He'd upset her, upset Wanda—his mind was warped, he knew that, he'd lived with it for long enough—and he couldn't be more pleased.

Joe Wilson's booted foot winged its way to Vance's stomach, and the *oof* of surprise that came out of him turned to a yell of anger. This wasn't between Vance and Joe, that man shouldn't be involved. This was between Vance and Wanda, no one else.

He blinked, focusing on the woman with the lovely tits, and she wasn't Wanda but Lou. "Did you breastfeed?" He smiled. Laughed a raspy laugh. Coughed.

Joe made a move to attack again, but Lou flashed out a hand to keep him back.

"No. Leave him." She gave Vance all of her attention. "You asked me that before. Why do you need to know?"

Vance spat out a tooth. Funny how he hadn't registered her fist breaking it loose at the time it had happened. Blood coated his tongue, the taste metallic. "Well, did you?"

Lou stared at him, disgust and misunderstanding twisting her features. "Yes."

"Then what I did…was justified."

He closed his eye, needing to shut her out for a moment.

"What the fuck do you mean?" Cassie. Sticking her oar in.

"You're sick in the head." Brenda, the one who'd wrecked his eye, lying, telling him she'd made a mistake and they belonged together.

Vance's face seemed as if it bloated right there and then, swelling, the skin tight. "I won't talk to you. To either of you. I've got nowt to say to Lenny's kid, nor to you, Brenda."

441

"Well, you'd better talk to someone," Cassie snapped. "Give these poor people some answers. An explanation."

Vance sighed. It was the end, he wasn't stupid, and he may as well tell them. At least it'd be out of his head for the scant time he suspected he had left. There was no way a Grafton would let him live, not now. He was lucky Cassie was on his case and not Lenny.

He opened his eye. "She suckled at your breast." He gazed at Lou. "I was jealous."

"You fucking *what*?" Joe, the man who probably had the pleasure of gnawing on her nipples of a night.

Lucky bastard.

"There were loads of them," Vance said. "All of them pissed me off, having what I couldn't. So I took them. Ended things for them."

He'd tried to hold it back, keep the urge inside him, for years and years, but when Jess had wandered along that alley at the edge of Old Barrington, he hadn't been able to hide the need any longer. Fury had taken over him.

He smiled, remembering, then sobered. If this was the end, he wouldn't have his angels with him like he'd planned. He'd painted eyes on them, the same as they'd looked on the real kids when he'd strangled them. Big and bulging. He'd written it into his will that he should be buried with them when he'd amended it last week to leave all his money to Brenda.

Oh God, she'd get the lot, the traitor.

The angels were back at the house, each glass figurine representing the girls he'd killed. He'd stopped them from becoming women who'd inevitably cut off their milk supply, stopped any children they'd have had suffering like him. Stopped all the mothers turning into Wanda.

He coughed again, his heart hurting, but not for what he'd done. No, it was sending out a warning signal: *Any more stress, and I'll stop beating*. "You wouldn't understand."

Lou stumbled in reverse, her back hitting the wall beside an old bookcase. She covered her chest, arms folded over them like they did to corpses in coffins, and he idly wondered whether a funeral parlour bloke would do that to him or if he'd meet that Marlene woman and be disposed of some other way.

Of course he would.

"Tell me she didn't suffer," Lou whispered. "That it was quick."

Vance copped sight of Brenda, who was crying, hugging herself as though that would bring her comfort. He shifted his sights to Joe. The man struggled to contain his anger, fists clenched, his red eyes showing he'd also been crying. Then Vance moved his attention to Cassie.

She glared at him: *Don't you dare tell her anything awful.*

He flicked to Lou again. She'd morphed into Wanda, and Vance smiled.

Said, "Oh, she suffered, and it wasn't quick."

A barbed *thing* came out of nowhere, lashing his face, spikes sticking into his skin. The pain was such that Vance couldn't bite down on the scream fast enough, and he roared, at the injustice, the unfairness of his life, the wickedness of his mother. The desperately lonely feelings he'd had throughout his childhood from six onwards, how he'd been gobsmacked when with women as to why he couldn't get any milk out.

Fuck. Fuck, he was so messed up, couldn't stand the confusion.

The barbs ripped out, and a strange sound came from his mouth. He peered through a watery eye at Joe, at him raising the evil weapon again, and Vance knew he'd experience a shedload of pain before he closed his eye for the final time.

He breathed deep and visualised his angels on the wall cabinet, recalling how he'd lovingly polished them, how they'd travelled with him in his lorry cab, stuck to the dash with Blu Tack.

He'd get to meet them for real soon, at Heaven's gates.

Although he acknowledged, as the barbs bit into him once more, he would likely end up in Hell with Wanda.

Another injustice.

Chapter Thirty

They stood around the body, all shocked, all silent. Cassie hated Vance for what he'd done, but especially that final admittance about Jess. He'd sent Lou and Joe on a new path of anguish, one where they'd imagine their daughter suffering. Thank God he hadn't described it, though that wouldn't lessen the torment. They could imagine well enough.

For want of something to say, she said, "We torched his bungalow before we left to come here. The police will think someone's going round burning old people's houses, what with the other one we set alight." She hated how business-like she'd sounded, how uncaring. Wished Dad hadn't taught her so well that she couldn't switch work off in a situation like this.

Lou swiped at her tears and stiffened her spine. "I want to watch him be put inside Marlene."

"Right. We'll go now." Cassie smiled, although it felt inappropriate, so she adopted her resting monster face.

"I want to push his head, feed him into the mincer," Lou said.

"Love, I don't think…" Joe sighed at his wife's dark expression. "Fine. If that's what you need."

"And I'm going to feed him to the pigs." Lou glared at the wreck on the floor. "He looks minced already."

And he did. Joe had done a massive number on him with the weapon. No part of Vance's body resembled a normal human. Almost all of his skin had been barbed, ripped, and he appeared as a lump of hacked meat strapped to a chair. Blood had flown, Vance's screams had echoed, and Lou's venomous words had ricocheted off the walls: "Fucking kill him. Murder the bastard. Hurt him. Let him feel my pain."

Cassie shivered at the memory. She'd never forget it, and going by the looks of things, Brenda would have nightmares for the rest of her life. The poor woman shook, her teeth chattering.

"No one, *no one* will know about this," Cassie said, and surprisingly, it was no longer important to her to hide Dad's error. This was about preserving Joe and Lou, and Brenda, ensuring they were never implicated in Vance's 'disappearance'. She turned to the married couple. "I don't want you caught. You don't deserve that."

Lou nodded, and Joe dipped his head.

"I don't regret it," he said. "I'd kill him a thousand times over, do time for him." He reached out to lay a hand on Brenda's shoulder. "Are you all right? Will you cope with this?"

Brenda nodded. "He was an animal."

Cassie took the weapon from Joe. "Then it's settled." She sighed. "We have work to do. There's Marlene to see and pigs to feed. Let's get to it."

Chapter Thirty-One

One Week Later

Cassie sat in the manager's office of the meat factory, Jason standing by the window behind her, peering out. A visibly broken Joe occupied the seat opposite, although his state might only be obvious to Cassie, knowing what she did. Jason wouldn't have a clue why Joe hunched instead of sitting straight, why his face had gained a few more wrinkles, the skin sagging. She'd asked him if he was sure about this, working as a manager part time, and he'd said he needed the distraction and, if he were honest, to have some time away from Lou during the day. Much as he loved her, he said her grief had come back full force, as if Jess had only been killed yesterday.

They waited for the only applicant to arrive, the man who'd share the responsibility with Joe. Cassie had looked him up in the RESIDENTS book, checking to see if he had any misdemeanours against his name. She'd never not look in that book now, not after the Vance bullshit.

He had no black marks and used to be an assistant manager at a Tesco Express.

A knock on the door had them all jumping, Jason moving from the window to stand by her side. He was there as an extra threat; the applicant would be made aware of who he was working for, although Cassie was confident enough in her abilities to think just *her* doing the interviewing would be adequate warning.

"Come away in," she said.

Marcus James entered the office, and his guts went south at the sight of Joe Wilson sitting there. Fuck, he was that nipper's dad, a man he'd avoided as much as possible over the years. Marcus would never forgive himself for being in the back of that van, had even taken to going to church, seeking the Lord as a way of shirking off any guilt. He hadn't done anything, not really, just hauled the kid inside and held her pinned to his lap until The Mechanic had driven them to his house, taking her inside while Alisha was at work.

Did Cassie know? Had she finally found out he'd been involved? Was this his day of reckoning, where not only God would know his part in that mess back then, but this lot, too? That Jason fella stood beside Cassie Grafton, his face stony, arms folded as if he stopped himself from grabbing a gun he was rumoured to carry and shooting Marcus right in the fucking head.

"Take a seat." Cassie stood to reach out for a handshake.

Marcus gripped her soft fingers and hoped she wouldn't feel his shaking. He let her hand go and all but fell into the chair beside Joe. Jesus Christ, he hadn't expected to be so close to the man ever again, not after that time in The Donny where Joe had been celebrating his birthday and offered Marcus a pint of beer. Marcus had pretended he was just off home. How could he sup a brew bought by the man of the dead child? God wouldn't like that. God would say Marcus had let the Devil in, accepting such a kind gesture.

"Okay, let's get this started." Cassie sat and jumped right in, reeling off the duties of the manager's position, stating Marcus would be working closely with Joe, splitting the job between them. "Joe will train you. Is that something you'd be happy with?"

Marcus swallowed. He wouldn't be, no, but what could he do? He'd been unemployed for so long, losing his previous job to the downscaling of staff, and he had a teenager to get through university in a few years. All right, his son would get a grant, but Marcus hadn't wanted him to rely solely on handouts.

"That's fine by me," he said.

"Full-time wages, as advertised," Cassie went on. "It's not your fault I decided to keep Joe on and split the hours."

She babbled a load of other stuff, shit Marcus couldn't take in. His mind was too full of how often he'd actually have to see Joe after the training was complete, how many conversations they'd have to have face to face. Could he handle that?

He closed his eyes and asked God, who replied that so long as Marcus had repentance in his heart, true sorrow for what he'd done, everything would be okay.

"So you can start tomorrow then?" Cassie asked.

Marcus nodded. "Yeah, I can start tomorrow."

But today he'd go to church, confess his sins, and promise to never, *ever* walk down the dark path again.

Chapter Thirty-Two

C assie stood with her back pressed to her bedroom door and let the tears fall. It had been a while since the last time she'd allowed herself to grieve, and the pressure of always appearing strong and in control had got to her.

Mam, it was Mam who'd set her off.

Earlier, when Cassie had walked in after interviewing Marcus James, she'd caught the sound of Mam's voice. Thinking she had a visitor, Cassie stowed her boots and coat away and ensured her gun was concealed in her jeans waistband beneath her top, telling herself to buy a bloody holster and be done with it.

"So I said to myself, 'Francis, keep it together for Cass. Once she's settled, once she can handle things by herself, I'll go to Lenny.' But that would be selfish, wouldn't it? Leaving her with no parents at all?"

Cassie's legs had gone, and she'd sagged against the hallway wall.

"So while I miss you, Len, I can't do it. I can't leave her."

Then the wailing had come, horrible heartfelt sobs that touched Cassie in a way the others hadn't. Mam was crying because she was torn.

She wanted to go to Dad, yet the kind nature she only showed Cassie wouldn't allow her to leave her behind. Her mother's instinct wouldn't allow it.

How Cassie had wished then, that Lenny Grafton hadn't had the idea of ruling the estate, his wife going along for the ride, their daughter dragged into it. How she wished she didn't have this burden of continuing his role, the expectation of it, the need to do it ingrained in her so deeply she wasn't sure she'd ever really wanted to be a teacher, the career she'd ditched in favour of…this.

And how she'd wished he hadn't died, leaving Mam in a tangle of private mourning so emotionally chaotic she couldn't see her way out of it. If Dad hadn't had the stress of a job he'd created in some mad bout of drunkenness with

Joe in The Donny, so the story went, his heart might not have given out on him.

Life would have been so different. For all of them.

She wiped her cheeks, rubbed her eyes, and sat on the bed. Her phone went off, and she was tempted to ignore it, but it was the work one, so she'd better look.

Jason: *Now things have calmed down a bit, fancy dinner in The Donny?*

Cassie sighed.

For fuck's sake. She'd go for this one meal, see how he was in a more relaxed setting, and ask herself one last time whether she wanted a relationship with him. He was a good-looking man, she certainly found him attractive, it was just his way, his pushy manner that put her off. Although…he'd stepped back a lot, allowed her to have the first and last say instead of him.

462

Allowed. Like he had a choice.

She thought about how they'd colluded to murder Nathan Abbott, how it had gone so well, the pair of them in sync. He had a point, they did seem to be destined to do that sort of shit together. Maybe it'd work outside the job, too?

Cassie: *Okay. One chance. I'll be there in half an hour. I need to go to the Jade first. Li Jun has something to report.*

Jason: *You won't regret it.*

She hoped not, but if she didn't give it a chance, she'd maybe always question herself later down the line. She could do with having Jason deeper in her pocket anyroad and, heartless as that sounded, she'd use him to her advantage.

I'm just like Brenda, using a man to get what I want.

She changed into something more in keeping with a date, if it could really be called that, and went downstairs to check on Mam. She was asleep in the armchair, Dad's favourite Fair Isle jumper clutched in her hands, and Cassie had to turn away or she'd lose it.

She drove to the Jade, switching her mind from the personal to business, and parked outside the Chinese. Li Jun had texted 'problem', and it reminded her that Doreen had messaged 'news' not an hour ago. Seemed Karen and Sharon *were* up to something, but Doreen couldn't work out what yet, and she'd need more time with them to suss it all out.

Fine by Cassie.

She got out of her car, engaged the locks, and approached the Jade, the darkness pierced by the bright lights from inside. No customers sat on the benches, which was odd, because the takeaway always had someone in it if the place was open. Li Jun wasn't behind the counter, neither were any of his family, and that was highly unusual. She pushed the door, but it didn't budge.

What the fuck was going on?

She took a bunch of keys from her pocket—Mam owned the Jade now, so Cassie was in charge of the place—and slid the right one into the lock. Inside, she ensured the keeper clicked into place, then approached the counter.

"Li Jun?" she called out, drumming her fingertips on the menu spread out beneath the glass top.

No answer.

She stared through the open square in the wall into the kitchen, but no one worked at the hobs, no woks full of chicken and noodles, no chef tossing them about. White water in a pan bubbled, steam rising, and she assumed it contained rice.

The kitchen was never left unattended.

Uneasy, she lifted the hatch and walked through, pressing on the swing door ahead and entering the kitchen. Words in Mandarin came, faint, a male, Li Jun if she was any judge. She'd heard him speak in his language often enough. Someone responded, a female, frantic, then a sob.

Cassie rushed past the cooking area towards another door that stood ajar. It led to the yard at the back, and the security light was on out there, although she couldn't see anyone. She slowed, her heart racing, her instincts picking up that there was more than a fucking 'problem'.

"Li Jun? It's me." She kicked the outer door, and it swung wide.

Li Jun stood there, his face spattered with blood. Cassie shot her attention to Yenay, Li Jun's niece, who crouched over someone else. And that someone else was Jiang, Yenay's brother, and he had his throat slit, scarlet soaking into his white chef jacket. Two more Chinese men stood to the right, Li Jun's sons, their jackets also smeared with the red stuff.

"Oh my fucking God, what the hell's happened?" Cassie asked.

"There is a war," Li Jun said. "Someone come, kill my nephew. It is the drugs. They wanted the drugs."

Cassie's skin went cold, and a rage so immense took over that she had trouble remaining calm. "Who was it?"

Li Jun shrugged. "I do not know, he had balaclava on, but when I find him, I use machete like he used. I slit *his* throat."

Cassie stood tall. "Not if I find him first."

Printed in Great Britain
by Amazon

20080033R00274